PRAISE FOR

THE GARDENER'S DAUGHTER

"*A Gardener's Daughter* calmly captivates from the beginning and develops characters we can all relate to. This beautiful story reminds us to take a deep breath, slow down, and reevaluate what is important to us in our lives. It left me with the feeling that life can be cherished if we take a second to actually enjoy it."

—**RACHAEL BROOKS,** Author of *Beads: A Memoir About Falling Apart and Putting Yourself Back Together Again*

"Powerful revelations of the driving force of memories. Negative memories, resulting from a lonely childhood, may become a positive force in motivating one to excel and succeed. Memories of the horrors of war may drive even the strongest down the path of desolation and destruction. The author allows us to exam true-to-life dilemmas brought about by memories. Encouragement and hope is found in the author's revelation of a well-worn path to a desirable and positive outcome."

—**CAPTAIN LARRY KENNETH HUNTER,** Author of *Fire Mission! Fire Mission!*

The Gardener's Daughter
by C.J. Foster

© Copyright 2019 C.J. Foster

ISBN 978-1-63393-880-9

Published by

 köehlerbooks™

210 60th Street
Virginia Beach, VA 23451
800—435—4811
www.koehlerbooks.com

THE GARDENER'S DAUGHTER

A NOVEL

C.J. FOSTER

VIRGINIA BEACH
CAPE CHARLES

To Dad. My hero.

CHAPTER ONE

FLOWERS WERE BUDDING EARLY, the gardener noticed with no small measure of satisfaction. The winter had been made more miserable by wet weather, but its moisture trapped deep in the soil spurred plants to bloom sooner than expected. As a result, Hope, Pennsylvania, looked lush with life this late-spring morning, and that was just fine by Joe Keller. Spring had always been his favorite time of the year. It made him think about new beginnings—rebirth; new life; hope for the future.

He had come out early to finish Mrs. Boudreaux's garden. Truth be told, he just liked being outside right after sunrise, especially this time of year. The crisp air refreshed Joe. Even after thirty years of working in landscaping, the beauty of life springing from the earth after a cold dormancy never ceased to amaze him. Spring was truly a magnificent time.

Kneeling on the moist, rich soil in Mrs. Boudreaux's side yard, Joe stopped unrolling landscape fabric to admire the first shrub he was about to place gently into its earthen cradle. *Mrs. Boudreaux will love these azaleas*, he thought. Joe had driven to a farm in Maryland that had the most beautiful azaleas he had ever seen north of the Mason-Dixon line, perfect for the Southern touch he needed to complete Mrs. Boudreaux's garden. They might not grow as tall in the cool Pennsylvanian air as they did in her native Georgia, but he hoped they would bring a bit of the South to her doorstep.

He wondered how many of Mrs. Boudreaux's neighbors, or the people in the cars driving by, would notice the sweet fragrances and vibrant colors filling the Pennsylvania landscape. If they didn't, Joe pitied them. He loved that his job put him in daily contact with such glories. It had not always been that way; as a younger man, he too would have overlooked the splendors of spring.

Anyone looking at Joe would think he was in remarkable health at sixty-eight. He was lean and strong; his full head of gray hair only added to what his wife, Audrey, called his "aura of distinction." Other than the high blood pressure he had developed while in the military, he had been blessed with good health. He no longer ran as much as he did in his youth, but he certainly got plenty of exercise digging, weeding and planting. Audrey had been begging him to retire for some years now, but Joe resisted.

"Twenty years in the Army, and decades more as a landscaper," she told him. "Don't you think it's time you stopped to smell the roses instead of planting them, Joe?"

"But that's what I do every day, love," he had replied. "It's good for the body and soul." She didn't know how true those words were for the old soldier. Joe meticulously covered the flower bed with the soft, gray matting he used to prevent weeds from overcoming Mrs. Boudreaux's little piece of Dixie. No patch was left unprotected. *Perfect,* he noted with a satisfied smile. It was time now for his favorite part of the job. The row of flowering bushes that would bring added serenity to Mrs. Boudreaux's yard were lined up and ready to be planted.

Still on his knees, Joe reached over the prepared ground, careful not to disturb the matting, and picked up the first plant. He was surprised by how heavy the container seemed. *That's odd.* He lifted such containers almost every day and had never noticed the weight before. As he lowered the plant, Mrs. Boudreaux's dainty white house spun. Joe's throat went dry as intense pounding in his head started.

Suddenly, horrid images of helicopters in the night flashed through his mind. He could hear the screams and smell the charred flesh of his friends burning in the wreckage like it was yesterday. These visions were no strangers to Joe, but this was the first time he had had one while he was awake. *Am I awake?* He tried to call out for help but didn't recognize his own voice. The only sounds that left his lips were garbled and unintelligible.

Joe struggled to his feet, but his left side was heavy. With all his might, he commanded his left arm to move, but it was no use. It hung by his side as if it was no longer attached to his body.

The world continued to spin. Joe lost his balance and fell to his side, right onto the azalea bush he was about to plant. Confused, he tensed his muscles and again tried to push himself up from the ground. It was useless. His left arm and leg felt as though they were stuck in quicksand.

Then he saw it. A single white flower, right in front of him. He focused on its beauty, and everything around it went dark. He could no longer smell the fragrance he had inhaled just a moment ago. All that remained was the vision of the soothing flower.

Calm overtook panic as he stared at the soft, white petals just inches from his face. Then that solitary image faded as well, leaving him in quiet darkness. Finally, even consciousness left him.

CHAPTER TWO

MASSACHUSETTS GENERAL HOSPITAL SAT in the middle of Downtown Boston. Each year its large, state-of-the-art emergency room logged a whopping 85,000 visits from people seeking care for everything from minor cuts to life-threatening events. The worst nights for physicians to be on call at a hospital were Thanksgiving, New Year's Eve, the Fourth of July, and, according to many superstitious doctors, nights with a full moon. The previous night was no exception; the bright moon had shone over a particularly busy night in the ER.

Shortly after eight on a Wednesday morning, Dr. Lauren Keller, attending physician in Internal Medicine, walked briskly through the bustling intensive care unit. Today would be an even busier day than normal, as her colleague, Dr. Rainey, had taken leave to attend to a family emergency. This meant that Laura had to cover his patients and check on the work of his residents—recent medical school graduates getting intense hands-on training.

Medical rounds occurred every morning on the hospital floors harboring patients. During rounds, the attending or staff physician and the new doctors gathered to discuss patient management plans. Rounds allowed the attending staff to gauge a resident's knowledge and teach them, while making sure that the patients continued to receive appropriate care.

Rounds for the ICU were slated for eight sharp, and the residents were surprised that Dr. Keller was a few minutes late. She prided herself on reliability and punctuality and often told the student doctors that she had never missed a shift. Even as a first-year resident suffering from the flu, she completed her call nights regardless of how sick she felt. To her mind, such dedication was required to be a great physician.

While attending Harvard's prestigious medical school, Lauren's classmates joked that while nuns dedicated their lives to Jesus, she dedicated her life to the medical school's hallowed hall. Lauren studied day and night, spending most of her free time in the anatomy lab dissecting cadavers and studying their preserved organs to try to figure out what pathology contributed to each corpse's demise. When not in the lab, she would stay up late in the library researching diseases and memorizing their symptoms, relevant diagnostic tests, and treatments.

Sure, it was a lonely existence, but one that paid dividends. Few students were selected for the three-year Internal Medicine residency program at Massachusetts General, and of those, only a smaller percentage received an invite to remain on as staff. At forty-three, Lauren was not only an attending physician in the Department of Internal Medicine at Mass General, but a full professor at Harvard Medical School. She embodied dedication and success, attributes she instilled by example into the young doctors-in-training under her charge.

This morning, however, Dr. Keller's thoughts were not entirely on her job as she prepared to make rounds. Her husband, Chris, had been supportive of her demanding profession for most of their marriage. But lately he had been pushing her to slow down and spend more time at home, despite her repeated explanations that her career was at a crucial point.

Things boiled over, and Chris told his wife he was leaving and had already rented a small apartment. Their six-year-old son, Joey, burst into tears and begged to stay with his dad. Lauren, swallowing her shock and dismay, said that it made more sense for Chris and Joey to remain in the family home and for her to live in the apartment. She moved that weekend amid a river of tears.

Lauren had fully expected that Chris would soon come to his senses and everything would return to normal. But her usually compliant husband remained steadfast. For the marriage to continue, Lauren had to change her workaholic ways, he insisted.

The previous night, Lauren arrived at her apartment late, as usual, failing to notice the official-looking envelope from a law firm until sorting her mail in the morning. The letter contained a statement of formal separation filed by Chris and informed Lauren that he was moving ahead with divorce proceedings. She'd sat hard upon reading the letter, overwhelmed and bitter. It had taken her some time to calm down enough to drive to work, and of course the delay meant she'd run into rush-hour traffic, causing her to arrive at the hospital later than usual. She hadn't even had time to swing by her office before heading straight to the ICU to begin her rounds.

She nodded curtly to the group of eight young doctors waiting, filled with disbelief that she was late. Dr. Keller dumped her briefcase and purse at the nurses' station and took the rolling stand with the laptop displaying the electronic medical records for the ICU patients. Her personal issues would wait. She needed to focus.

Standing in the hall outside the first room, Dr. Keller scrolled through the record of a patient while the residents waited. Some of the residents shifted nervously as Dr. Keller frowned.

"Dr. Sutton. Did anything strike you as odd about our patient in bed one?"

Dr. Faye Sutton's big blue eyes bulged with apprehension. The petite, pretty strawberry blonde had been a resident for nearly a year at Mass Gen, yet this was her first day on rounds with the notorious Dr. Keller. When she heard that Dr. Rainey had to take some days off, Faye had prayed that any attending physician other than Dr. Keller would be filling in. Her fellow residents had warned Faye about *Dr. Terminator*, the nickname that captured both Dr. Keller's reputation for dismissing ill-prepared interns from the residency program and her unrelenting, robotic work ethic and incredible depth of medical knowledge. Her ability to quickly and accurately diagnose patients' maladies was legendary at the hospital—as was her quick temper.

Faye had been a star student in college and medical school, but so had all the other residents in her new peer group. For the first time in her life, Dr. Sutton was finding that she had to work harder than the rest of the group to keep up. That meant coming into the hospital at three in the morning—as she had this morning—to gather all the information on the dozen or so critical patients in the unit. Four new patients had been admitted that morning, and Dr. Sutton frantically compiled vital signs and medication lists and memorized the notes from the emergency room staff. If called upon, she would be expected to accurately regurgitate all the necessary information to the attending physician.

Dr. Keller's cool so unnerved Dr. Sutton that she did not quite hear the question and blurted out her prepared summary of the case.

"Um, Mr. Szary presented to the ER in diabetic ketoacidosis earlier this morning. Signs included ptosis and right-sided facial droop, which could indicate a stroke. His blood sugars were in the 500s. I started him on an insulin drip and had him transferred to the ICU. He responded very well and his glucose is now stable at 125. Non-contrast CT didn't show a bleed, so I put in a call for a neurology consult to see about initiating tPA therapy," Faye methodically reported.

"Did you notice that the patient also complained of a headache and his CT showed mild mucosal thickening of the ethmoid sinus?" asked Dr. Keller.

"Yes, Doctor," Dr. Sutton replied, hiding her shaking hands in the pockets of her white coat. She nervously wondered why Dr. Keller was concerned about the sinus findings on the patient's computed tomography report.

"The ER notes also say that Mr. Sary also had some eye symptoms," Dr. Keller continued.

"Actually, ma'am, his name is *Szary*, not *Sary*. The *Sz* makes a *Sh* sound. It's Ukrainian, I think."

The other interns and residents on the team froze. Only their eyes moved to look at each other. Faye noticed two nurses at the nurses' station grin at each other before raising their gazes to Dr. Keller. A first-year resident correcting Dr. Terminator? The young resident swallowed and braced herself.

Lauren shook her head. She was more disappointed than angry—with herself.

Lauren had heard Dr. Rainey praise Dr. Sutton's compassion and contagious, upbeat demeanor. The young resident was smart and well liked, but Lauren now wondered whether her medical skills were as sharp as purported.

Dr. Keller said drily, "I am glad to see you've mastered *some* aspects of this case, Dr. Sutton, but when evaluating patients during admission into the ICU, it's necessary to prioritize what needs attention first. *Life*-threatening signs and symptoms."

Dr. Sutton flushed red. Dr. Keller noticed the resident shoot an appealing glance at Dr. Aaron Shalle, the chief resident, who responded, "Mr. Szary's glucose levels are now stable, Dr. Keller. He's on an insulin drip and doing well. Neurology is on the way to evaluate him about the extent of his stroke."

Dr. Keller turned her gaze on the tall, brown-skinned young man. She was fond of Aaron. He had overcome great obstacles to emigrate to the United States from Ethiopia. His perseverance and hard work had made him one of the best residents in the program, earning him the coveted position of chief resident in his third year. But at the moment, his ready defense of Dr. Sutton nettled Dr. Terminator, inflaming her suspicions of Dr. Sutton's evaluative skills.

"That's all good and well, Dr. Shalle, and I appreciate your attentiveness to Dr. Sutton's patient, but you won't always be there to take care of her patients for her. Besides, Mr. *Szary* needs ENT more than he needs neurology right now." Lauren glared at Dr. Sutton.

"But he had a stroke," Dr. Sutton faltered. "Isn't that the highest priority after treating the DKA?"

"What was the cause of the stroke?" Lauren asked in a quiet but deliberate tone. Dr. Shalle and the other residents watched her attentively, knowing the unflappable Dr. Keller was about to impart a lesson.

"Well, he's seventy-two years old with multiple cardiovascular risk factors including uncontrolled diabetes and high blood pressure," countered Dr. Sutton. "All of which probably contributed."

"So, you assumed. However, stroke doesn't cause sinus thickening and a swollen eyelid," Dr. Keller insisted.

"Oh, that. Well, I thought that, um, a swollen eye coupled with a frontal headache and the sinus thickening were just signs of sinus trouble or allergies," Dr. Sutton said.

"More assumptions," Lauren retorted. "I don't see anything in the notes about a history of allergies. Have you ever heard of *mucormycosis*, Dr. Sutton?"

"Uh. No," the resident replied, her voice cracking.

Dr. Keller glanced at the other residents. "Anyone?"

Dr. Shalle nodded. "I've heard of it. Something to do with an infection. There are a few variants, if I recall. One can enter through the nose and infect the brain."

Dr. Keller flashed a rare smile. "Very good, Doctor.

Mucormycosis is sometimes found in immunocompromised patients. It's caused by a fungus from the mucoraceae family. Symptoms depend on the site of the body that the fungus invades. Although rare, rhinocerebral mucormycosis is the variant most discussed in the medical literature. It's also very deadly. Your patient showed the classic signs of this invasive fungal infection, Dr. Sutton, from the frontal sinus headache and eye swelling to the CT findings and the stroke, which can happen in rhinocerebral mucormycosis. His uncontrolled diabetes contributed to his weakened immunity and made him more susceptible to the infection."

"But his presentation was textbook for a thrombotic stroke," Dr. Sutton said.

"Diseases don't read textbooks, Dr. Sutton," Dr. Keller chastised. "It's not enough to learn just the facts about diseases. You also need to use your brain to analyze the clinical findings and uncover the true source of the pathology."

Lauren turned to Dr. Shalle. "Call ENT and tell them what we suspect. Order an MR spectroscopy. We also need labs and cultures, and get some Amphotericin B up from the pharmacy right away.

Dr. Keller turned her gaze on the now flushed Dr. Sutton.

"Mr. *Szary* needs to be prepped for the OR for sinus debridement before the fungus spreads throughout his brain. We've already lost enough time focusing on the wrong diagnosis. Oh, and, Dr. Sutton . . . cancel the neuro consult."

Dr. Sutton's eyes swelled, fighting back tears of embarrassment. Had her misdiagnosis actually put Mr. Szary's life in peril? She blinked, and then jumped as a gentle hand was placed on her shoulder.

"*Mucormycosis?*" a voice asked from behind her.

The resident turned to see the director for Clinical Services, Dr. Carl Russell, who smiled at her. Dr. Sutton meekly smiled back. His presence and demeanor reminded her of her father, a well-known plastic surgeon from Manhattan. Like her father, Dr. Russell was strong yet caring. His quiet, even humble manner coupled with his brilliance as a diagnostician had earned the respect of all who worked with him.

"My, my," the director said softly. "I haven't seen that for years. Quite rare," he added, coming to stand beside Dr. Sutton but looking at the residents. "Now, why do you think Dr. Keller wants an MR spectroscopy rather than just an ordinary MRI?"

Dr. Keller smiled at her mentor and raised her eyebrows at the residents, indicating that she too was waiting to hear the answer.

Dr. Shalle was the first to provide one. "Spectroscopy will measure the chemical metabolism that's occurring in the brain tissue."

"True," answered Director Russell. He looked at Dr. Sutton. "And how can this help us determine that *mucormycosis* caused Mr. Szary's stroke rather than the embolus that we might logically expect in a man with the cardiovascular risk factors you identified in your presentation of this case?"

Dr. Keller watched as Dr. Sutton pulled herself together and put her mind to work on the question, admiring as she so often had Director Russell's knack for bringing out the best in students, just as he had with her all those years ago when she was a young resident in this same ICU.

"The spectroscopy will show biochemical markers related to an organism that wouldn't be there in a regular, embolic stroke?" Sutton answered, somewhat timidly.

"You are correct, Dr. Sutton. Very good. And by comparing the profiles of these different biochemical markers in suspicious cases, you can rule out or rule in some of the less common causes of stroke." He smiled at the residents. "This case is a perfect example of how one must always keep one's mind open to every possible diagnosis, no matter how *textbook* the presentation might be. This is what physicians mean when we talk about the art of medicine. Now, let's go in and see our patient, shall we?"

The residents followed the director into the room, but Lauren detained the chief resident. "Dr. Shalle, a word please?"

The two walked down the hall.

"Do you think you're doing Dr. Sutton any favors by protecting her when she makes a mistake?"

"I did not—"

"You did. When she was in trouble, she looked to you to save her, and you jumped right in. Dr. Sutton's never going to be a good doctor if she gets in the habit of depending on others. Especially if she uses her physical attractiveness, even unconsciously, to get help.

I suggest that you put a stop to this right away and make her stand on her own two feet."

"With all due respect, Dr. Keller, I think you've misread the situation," Dr. Shalle answered stiffly. "I've worked with Dr. Sutton all year, and I do not think she depends on others. Nor am I susceptible to such manipulation, as you imply."

Lauren looked at him for a long moment.

"I'm glad to hear it, if that's true. Well, let's get back to rounds."

As she turned, she saw Faye Sutton slip into Mr. Szary's room. No doubt she'd been at the nurses' station cancelling the neuro consult. Lauren felt momentarily disquieted, but then decided that if Dr. Sutton had overheard her conversation with Dr. Shalle, it might be a good thing.

CHAPTER THREE

LAUREN STOOD IN LINE with her longtime friend and mentor at the coffee shop in the sprawling Massachusetts General complex.

"Carl, they're just not prepared enough for rounds," she huffed. It had taken her over three hours to get through morning rounds in the two intensive care units. "You heard how some of them are struggling with basic medicine concepts. Medicine isn't a job—it's a calling. The residents need to read, be better prepared, and think more."

"I think you're being a little too hard on them, Lauren," the director said. "I certainly wouldn't label a complicated and rare case such as a stroke caused by rhinocerebral mucormycosis *basic*. And to be honest with you, I probably would have missed Mr. Szary's diagnosis as well. I think I've only seen two or three cases of it in my entire career."

"That's not the point," Lauren said, embarrassed by the reproach from her mentor. Despite holding one of the most powerful positions in the hospital, Carl remained as kind and nurturing to Lauren as he had when she was a resident here. And Lauren had never lost her desire to shine in his eyes.

"Different students require different teaching methods. Dr. Shalle does well with your usual tell-it-like-it-is approach, just as you did when I was teaching you. But some students do better with gentler guidance," Carl said.

Lauren knew Carl was talking about Dr. Sutton, but his words struck home. One of the issues her husband had brought up when they separated was how strict she was with their six-year-old son. Lauren had to admit to herself that her relationship with Joey was not nearly as strong as she had hoped for. In fact, it was almost nonexistent. *Is that why Joey decided to live with his father?* she wondered.

Lauren knew that her work came between her and her family at times. It wasn't just the long hours she put in at the hospital; she was also doing research and teaching courses at Harvard. The problem, Lauren felt, was that Chris just didn't comprehend the enormous responsibility she had, dealing with life and death on a daily basis. She loved Chris and Joey, but being a good doctor often seemed incompatible with being a good wife or parent. Her mother, Audrey, had succeeded as a wife and mother by devoting herself to her family. She had a successful career as a counselor but had only worked part-time until Lauren went off to college.

But Lauren didn't have that luxury. If she wanted to advance in her career, Lauren *had* to put that first. The morning rounds with the residents always reminded her she had to remain razor-focused.

Chris understood that in the earlier days of their marriage; he volunteered to be the stay-at-home parent so that Lauren could pursue her calling. He had even abandoned a career of his own, giving up his dream of becoming a computer engineer after Joey was born. Instead, he opted for a low-paying job where he could work from home, troubleshooting network problems for a medium-sized computer firm. It was a decent job, but Lauren had always felt guilty that Chris settled for less than he deserved. Chris was very bright and could have done much more with his life. But Chris never seemed to mind, and Lauren knew it was a good thing that he could be home with Joey when she could not. He had chosen a reward much greater than money or prestige: a strong relationship with his son.

But now Chris wanted things to change. He wanted a marriage, and a loving companion, not just someone who paid the bills and dashed off to work. *Doesn't he understand how much I'd have to give up to meet that demand?* Lauren wondered.

As Carl ordered his latte, Lauren's smartphone chimed. Dr. Shalle texted that Mr. Szary's scan had confirmed her diagnosis of mucormycosis. As she closed the message, the image on her phone's wallpaper—her family's Christmas picture from last year, taken on a ski trip to Vermont—flashed onto the screen. For the first time, she noticed the sullen expression on Chris's face.

She remembered that day. Chris had tried to get her to take time off for an extended vacation, but Lauren had resisted, citing personnel shortages at work. She finally agreed to a three-day weekend. They'd skied together one day. On the second day Lauren claimed she was too tired to ski and told Chris to take Joey to his skiing lessons while she relaxed in the lodge. Chris saw right through her. He accused her of wanting to stay back to work, which led to another fight.

She stared at the image and noticed that Joey wasn't smiling either. In fact, he wasn't even looking at the camera. Instead, he stared down at his shoes. *How did I not notice that before now?* she wondered. *Is he depressed, and I've missed the signs?* She looked back at Chris's face. He had aged in the past few years. His brown hair now had flecks of gray, and she noticed the beginnings of a receding hairline. *Still handsome, though,* she thought, as nearly forgotten emotions stirred deep inside her heart.

She stepped up to the counter as Carl took his latte from the woman at the register with a smile and a word of thanks. The woman replied, "My pleasure, Dr. Russell," with an answering smile. The exchange did not surprise Lauren. Carl was such a warm and patient man. Not only was he an excellent mentor, astute clinician, and beloved staff member, he was an ordained Baptist minister who routinely used his fatherly skills to heal hearts and minds as well as bones and lacerations. Every time she saw Carl, he was talking to someone, giving advice or just asking about their day. When she needed to consult with him, she usually had to wait for him to finish conversing with a medical student, coworker, or patient. It was rare for her not to hear laughter emanating from the office or patient room as she waited.

Lauren asked for her usual, black coffee, and could not help but observe that the woman's smile faded as she repeated Lauren's order in a mechanical tone.

"How do you do it, Carl?" she asked, turning to him.

"Do what?" he replied, sipping his latte.

Lauren wasn't sure herself what she was asking.

"You've achieved so much, not just in medicine, but in life. And you always remain positive and upbeat. And kind. How?"

"Oh, it's not that hard, Lauren. I surround myself with family, good friends, and caring colleagues. It's not a difficult recipe for success," he said, rubbing his hand over his neatly trimmed gray Afro. "That's the key."

Lauren had friends, but they were few. Even as a child, she preferred the company of books over people, especially during her early years when her father was deployed in some foreign land on another military mission. Her aunt Joanna would take her to the library every Saturday.

Books enabled Lauren to journey into a different world—one of science and discovery. Joey, it occurred to her, was quite the opposite. He was outgoing and loved the outdoors. He would rather play in the yard or hang out with his friends than read a book. *Perhaps he gets that from his father.* Chris was gregarious, had a wide circle of friends and loved the outdoors.

"You and Doreen have been married for, what, forty years?" Lauren asked Carl.

"Forty-one next September," he said. His eyes brightened at the name of his beloved wife.

"That's amazing," Lauren replied, sipping her hot beverage as she and Carl walked slowly down the busy hospital corridor. "I guess what I really want to know, is how do you find the time to be so . . . so focused on *people*? In a social way, I mean. And still have time to do your job?"

Carl smiled. "Well, I happen to think that *is* part of the job."

"Yes, but doesn't it distract you from the problem at hand, sometimes? I mean, from the signs and symptoms of their disease?"

Carl stopped and their eyes locked. "Lauren, you're a brilliant physician in terms of being an astute diagnostician, researcher, and yes, even teacher. But that's not all you need to be a good *doctor*. Compassion, for instance, can often help people heal in ways medicine cannot. I can't prove that scientifically, but I *know* it to be true. It takes a diverse, well-rounded team to do what we do here at the General. We all have our own strengths and weaknesses. That's what makes us who we are, and that's a good thing."

Carl turned the conversation to the current situation with the medical residents.

"You know, Lauren, Dr. Sutton is a thoughtful young woman. She's a fine doctor and cares deeply about her patients. Her compassion for her patient drives her to find answers to their ailments. It's compassion that will make her a fine doctor."

Lauren stiffened. "But compassion is not enough, Carl. A physician has to dedicate themselves to their craft. She has to be willing to put in the hours to learn disease processes in order to help people. Her diagnostic skills need improvement. She knows it, too. I could see her panicking today when she realized that she'd made decisions based on a lot of unfounded assumptions. And her first reaction was to look to Aaron for help. Carl, you know medicine is not for the faint of heart."

"Nor is it for the heart of stone, my dear."

Rarely could anyone wound her with words, but Carl wasn't just anyone; he was her mentor, her role model, her teacher and mostly a trusted friend. *His* words mattered. Did he truly think she was cold hearted? Stubbornly, she rallied.

"That patient could have died, you know? Early recognition and treatment for mucormycosis is key to survival."

"Yes. But he *didn't* because of you, and Aaron and our protocols. She's learning, Lauren, just as you did. Mistakes are only mistakes when they're not caught. And mistakes provide opportunity for improvement if you treat them as lessons."

"In medicine, we live in absolutes, Carl. There are no second chances. Our patients' lives depend on it. Treatment protocols exist for a reason."

"You're right. Yet *our* lives depend on the conditional. Uncertainty is inherent in the world. It's how we live our lives that makes us able to overcome uncertainty. There are positive and negative forces in nature, Lauren. I believe the positive forces are stronger, more effective. Use these, and the absolutes will come. Remember, my dear, you attract more bees with honey than vinegar." He finished with a warm smile.

Lauren couldn't help but return the smile, although she wasn't convinced. But her smile faded as Carl added, "Enough philosophy from an old man. I'm afraid I have some news that may not sit well with you." Lauren tensed. Still, she was unprepared for his next words. "I'm stepping down as director of Clinical Services, effective immediately."

"But *why?*" Lauren blurted, stopping dead in the middle of the hall. "Why would you do that? You're not even sixty-five yet. You have years of good work ahead of you."

The signature warm smile returned to Carl's weathered face.

"As you know, Lauren, I now have three grandchildren. It's time Doreen and I spent some more time with them."

"But what about the hospital? We need you here."

"Rubbish," he said with a grimace. "Harvard Medical School and Massachusetts General Hospital were here long before Dr. Carl

Darnell Russell Jr. arrived and will be here long after I have departed. It's time for me to move on, Lauren."

Lauren wanted to keep arguing, but Carl's expression suggested it would be fruitless. "Who is being considered for DCS?" she asked.

"The decision's been made already. Dr. Novotny. She is next in line for directorship."

Although Anna Novotny was ten years her senior, the two had been friends since Lauren arrived at Mass General. In many ways, they were alike. Both were strong, competitive, and independent. But Anna was a good administrator, a people person who was well liked by the hospital staff and residents. She was also an accomplished and respected clinician and researcher. From conversations with her, Lauren suspected that Anna also had a healthy relationship with her husband and two adult children. She quelled a sudden feeling of jealousy.

"She's a great choice!"

"Yes, I think so. And I also think you'd make a great chair of the internal medicine department when Anna vacates that position to take my place. It's only my recommendation, mind you. Dr. Novotny, as the new DCS, will make the final decision, of course."

Elation filled Lauren. The internal medicine department was a large and influential component of MGH. Being chair of the department had provided both Carl and Anna with the check in the box they needed to move up the hospital ladder. It was an honor that she'd hoped would come to her someday, but she'd never dreamed it would happen this soon.

"Carl, I don't know what to say. I won't let you down."

"I know you won't let me down, dear. But don't let *them* down," he said, pointing to a small group of residents walking ahead of them. "They need you to be their teacher, their counselor, their mentor and, at times, their friend. Medicine is more than memorizing facts, Lauren. You are a wonderful physician. Now, be the wonderful leader that I know you can be."

Lauren pondered these words. All her life, she had taken the reins of every situation. She had been class president and valedictorian in high school, graduated at the top of her class at Princeton, and was the head of Harvard's prestigious Alpha Omega Alpha Honor Society in medical school.

Leader! I am a leader, aren't I? she thought.

Lauren's phone rang before she could ask Carl to explain.

"I'll catch up with you later, Lauren."

Lauren pulled the phone out of her white lab coat.

"Lauren?"

The voice was weak, but Lauren instantly recognized it.

"Mom? What's wrong?" All she heard was sobbing. "Mom, talk to me. What is it?"

She heard a gulp. "Honey, it's your father. He's had a stroke."

"Dad? Is he at the hospital? How is he?" she asked, covering her other ear to help her hear in the noisy hallway.

"He's in the ICU. Dr. Spiva says it's bad. Can you come home? Lauren, are you there?"

Lauren shook herself out of her thoughts. "Yes, Mom. I'm here. I'll be there as soon as I can."

Chapter Four

AUDREY KELLER SAT IN the ICU room, listening to the rhythmic beeps coming from the many machines and monitors hooked up to her husband. Although friends, family, and hospital staff had been visiting all afternoon, Audrey felt alone. She and Joe had been apart many times during their forty-four-year marriage; he'd even been hospitalized before with a bad case of pneumonia and stayed in this very same intensive care unit. But this time she couldn't shake her fear that Joe would never wake up from his stroke-induced coma.

Joe was never one to sit in one spot very long. He was always on his feet, fixing things around the house, visiting friends, or walking with Audrey around the neighborhood. He was in such good shape. *How could this happen to him?* she wondered.

Glancing at the phone, she thought of the call she made to her daughter earlier. Lauren was their only child and the light of her father's eye. Audrey was glad she was coming home. Maybe the sound of his daughter's voice would help bring Joe back to them.

The last time Joe was hospitalized, Lauren had just finished residency and taken a staff position at Massachusetts General Hospital. From his hospital bed, with oxygen flowing into his nose through a nasal cannula, Joe told his daughter he understood why she couldn't come visit him. When he hung up the phone, however, Audrey saw the disappointment in his eyes.

They were both immensely proud of Lauren. But Audrey was concerned about her workaholic daughter. Her drive and determination brought her success, but Audrey sensed it put a strain on her marriage to Chris and perhaps even her relationship to her son, Joey. It was all intuition on Audrey's part; Lauren was not one for revealing her heart, even to her mother.

Lauren never had many real friends growing up, possibly because of the numerous moves they had to endure while Joe was in the Army. But even after Joe retired and the family settled in Joe's hometown of Hope, Pennsylvania, Lauren never really let anyone get close to her. In fact, the close relationship she had with her father as a child soured after Joe retired from the military. Some of that, Audrey knew, might have been normal adolescent rejection or, most likely, Lauren's resentment that her father was gone much of the time. Audrey had hoped the coolness between them would thaw over time.

Audrey sat in the recliner but couldn't relax. The stress of waiting was starting to get the best of her. The worst part was knowing there was nothing she could do, except to hold Joe's hand and talk to him, even though he probably couldn't hear her.

She rose with relief to greet Dr. Doug Spiva as he entered the room. Doug was not only their family physician but a good friend, and Audrey's trust in him was absolute. Doug moved to the bedside as a stocky man followed him into the room and immediately enveloped Audrey in a tight hug.

"What a shock," the gray-haired, overweight man murmured. "How are you doing?"

"Oh, Harry. I just never expected this," Audrey replied. "You know your brother. Joe's always been so strong, so healthy . . . it just doesn't make sense."

"I know, Audrey. It's hard to believe. Joanna sends her love and will come by tomorrow, but says to call if you need her," Harry Keller said, giving her a pat on the back before releasing her and approaching the bed.

Joe's younger brother looked nothing like him except for his eyes, which held the same intelligent warmth. Now they were filled with concern as he gazed upon Joe and then to the doctor, who finished checking Joe's vitals and now glanced over his medical chart.

"What's the word, Doc?"

Dr. Spiva shook his head. "No change. I'm sorry."

"I'm not clear on what happened," Harry said. "Audrey said he was not found for hours?"

"Yes," the doctor answered. "He was working in someone's garden when he had the stroke. He was hidden from the road by some bushes. The homeowner found him when she came out to collect her mail around one. From what we can tell, he may have been there six or seven hours."

Audrey sat heavily. "Oh, my poor Joe. I can't bear to think of him lying on the cold ground for so long."

"Fortunately, the weather today was mild, or we'd probably be dealing with pneumonia on top of everything else. But there's a window of time when we can do a lot to neutralize the damaging effects of a stroke. Unfortunately, we didn't get to him in time for that."

Audrey looked at him beseechingly. "But, Doug, there's still hope, isn't there?"

Dr. Spiva took her hand. "Audrey, I've always been honest with you and Joe, and I won't lie to you. Things don't look good. Joe may wake up again, or he may not. Even if he does, there's a good possibility that he will have quite a bit of impairment." He paused. "Is Lauren coming?"

"Yes," Audrey whispered. "She's catching a plane this evening."

"That's good," Doug answered.

Harry turned to Audrey. "You look beat. Why don't you go home for a while? I'll stay with Joe. Nothing's going to change anytime soon, is it, Doc?"

Dr. Spiva shook his head. "I doubt it. Harry's right, Audrey, you need a break. Go home, eat something, maybe take a nap, and come back in a couple of hours. We'll be here and let you know if anything changes, but I'd be surprised if it does."

Audrey resisted, but Harry eventually convinced her to leave the hospital. The drive home passed in a blur; her thoughts were with her husband as she traversed the familiar streets on autopilot. As she pulled into the driveway, the sight of the many bushes and flowers meticulously placed around the foundation of the house and at the edges of the neat lawn reminded her of how well Joe had kept his promise to her made all those years ago. A promise to make hers the most beautiful garden in town. The garden never failed to bring her peace and comfort, even at this moment.

She got out of the car and walked slowly around the yard. She noticed the early growth on the flame acanthi Joe had planted just a few days earlier, hoping to attract more butterflies to the garden. Audrey imagined how they would flutter and swoop about the blooms. Joe was right—gardens did add something to the world. They connected people with something primeval, something basic in life. All too often, people got lost in the bustle of the modern world. "We all need things to ground us," Joe was fond of saying. Audrey's mind jumped to her daughter. *What grounds Lauren?* Audrey wasn't sure.

As she stepped onto the porch and saw honeysuckle climbing up a lattice on one side of the porch, planted there by Joe for its beautiful scent, tears welled. She could imagine butterflies dancing and the smell of honeysuckle, but she couldn't imagine life without her husband. Sure, they had their ups and downs in their long marriage, but there were more happy memories than not, and the last twenty years had been the best.

Ever since Joe retired from the military and started his own landscaping business, he had seemed so happy and content. Year after year, he seemed brighter to her, as if he had exorcised most of the demons from his past. She thought about the trip they made to Maine two summers ago, during which they had hiked up a small mountain. Sitting on the summit, looking out over a beautiful sunrise, Joe suddenly turned to her and said, "I've never felt so alive!" They'd sat there for hours, enjoying the glory of the scenery and their happiness in each other.

In the first years of their marriage, Joe had been all about following the rules, keeping to the schedule, doing things the traditional way. But after he retired and brought his wife and daughter back to his hometown, he became so spontaneous, so full of life. He still had the bad dreams, but they became fewer and farther between. He loved his job and his community. It seemed to Audrey that he was friends with everyone in town. The couple couldn't go for a walk without someone stopping to say hello, or to thank Joe for the beautiful garden he had planted for them or for some other little favor he'd done.

Everyone seemed to appreciate Joe—except for his daughter.

Audrey had both an undergraduate and master's degrees in counseling psychology and understood why the teenage Lauren might have resented all the years her father spent overseas, away from his family. But Audrey felt it was long past time for her highly educated and accomplished daughter to realize that she was now behaving just like her father once had, putting her own profession before her family. How ironic that Lauren resented her father for being absent and, perhaps, choosing a new career that kept him closer to home.

Audrey had always regarded Lauren as very much her father's daughter, but there were differences. They both were passionate in everything they did, but Lauren was ambitious and sought prestige while Joe was humbler. Lauren wanted to save lives, not just one at a time but thousands through her work and research, while Joe concentrated on making life better for those around him in little ways, creating beautiful gardens or just saying hello and smiling at people he saw on the street.

As a mother, Audrey wanted her daughter not just to succeed but to be loved by those around her. *But do they? Do her patients even* like *her?* she wondered.

Audrey stood alone in a dark kitchen, thinking about her life. It had been wonderful by and large. But the two most important people to her remained estranged from one another. Alienated by their pride. Too stubborn to see that they were, in fact, more alike than either of them realized. Would there be enough time for them to open their eyes and see the truth?

CHAPTER FIVE

AS SHE PROMISED HER mother, Lauren did her best to leave work early. However, each time she tried, another crisis emerged. First, there were some new hospital admissions the residents seemed unable to handle on their own, so Lauren had to go down to the wards to help them manage the sicker patients. In the afternoon, she had a research review board to chair. She did manage to table some of the agenda to a later date, but despite her efforts, the meeting ran late. Then there was the stack of patient charts to read and sign off on, a daily chore that could not be avoided. She was just about to call Anna Novotny to tell her that she needed to take some time off when the new DCS knocked on her door and took a seat.

Lauren remembered her manners and congratulated her friend on her promotion. Anna nodded her thanks, then said without preamble, "Unfortunately the promotion means I have responsibility for some unpleasant tasks, Lauren. I'm afraid I have to tell you that there's been a complaint lodged against you."

"Oh God, not another one," Lauren blurted out. "A nurse?"

Someone from the nursing staff recently filed a complaint about Lauren's brusque manner, accusing her of not respecting either the nurses' knowledge or their authority. Lauren had countered that respect had nothing to do with it; as attending physician the ultimate responsibility for her patients lay with her, not the nurses, and they were duty bound to follow her orders.

"No. One of the residents. Dr. Sutton. Is it true you accused her of using her sexuality to manipulate the male doctors?"

"What? That's nonsense, Anna. The only thing I've accused Dr. Sutton of is jumping to conclusions instead of looking at all the data before diagnosing a patient."

Anna frowned. "I misspoke. She said you accused her of such behavior, but not to her face, to another resident, and she overheard you. I asked the other resident and he confirms that you did say something to that effect."

Et tu, Aaron? Lauren thought with bitterness. "I did mention to Dr. Shalle that he seemed overprotective of Dr. Sutton. As I said, she had misdiagnosed a patient, and I wanted her to learn from the incident. She'll never become a good doctor if others cover for her mistakes."

"And did you suggest that Dr. Shalle was motivated to do so because he is attracted to Dr. Sutton?"

Lauren paused, trying to recall the conversation, which now seemed ages ago.

"Not that exactly. What I saw was Dr. Sutton making doe eyes at Dr. Shalle when she didn't know the answer to my questions, and he immediately stepped in to save her. I warned him against that kind of thing. I said nothing to Dr. Sutton herself. Her behavior is Dr. Rainey's concern, not mine."

"Yes, exactly," Anna said. "You should have shared such a concern with him, or with me, if it seemed that serious to you. Unfortunately, no one else who has worked with Dr. Sutton has seen any such behavior. I'm afraid it looks like you're the one who jumped to conclusions, Lauren. What makes it worse is that Faye Sutton is claiming that some of the nurses have told her you, uh, 'have it in' for younger, prettier women. If others confirm this, there could be grounds for a harassment case here."

Lauren, stunned, could only stammer. "Come on, Anna, that's ridiculous."

Anna shrugged. "I agree, but it doesn't help that the nurse who filed that other complaint is, in fact, young and quite attractive. To make things worse, Faye's dad is Dr. Richard Sutton, who happens to be good friends with the CEO of Mass General. He has heard about the incident and is pushing for an investigation."

I'll bet Faye Sutton called him right away, Lauren thought. "Daddy protecting his little girl?"

"I know," Anna acknowledged. "I spoke to Carl about this and he called the CEO on your behalf and warned that Dr. Sutton Senior running interference for his daughter would only confirm your impression that Faye expects men to take care of her. Either way, Lauren, I've been tasked with resolving the situation. Hopefully I can keep it from becoming a matter for the board." She sighed. "I'll warn you, Lauren, you'll probably have to apologize, and there's a good chance you'll have to go through some kind of awareness training."

Lauren grimaced. *As if I have time for such nonsense.* "I have to ask. I know Carl's put my name up for head of Internal Med. Does this jeopardize my chances?"

Anna looked away. "First things first. Let me deal with this complaint, and then we'll talk about your future at Mass Gen." She started to rise, then looked more closely at Lauren and sat back down.

"What is it? I've never seen you look so rattled. It's not just this complaint, is it?"

"No, it's not that," Lauren admitted. "I just found out my dad had a stroke. I was just going to call you, in fact. I need to go home for a day or two." *Not to mention that my husband wants a divorce,* she thought. That was news she wasn't ready to discuss with Anna—or anyone else.

Anna laid a hand on Lauren's. "Oh, I'm so sorry. Is it bad?"

"I'm not sure. My mom said it was, but I need to see him and the labs and films. I wish we had him here, instead of that Podunk little hospital where they live."

"Well, if you think he'd be better off here, we can find a bed," Anna said. "And you know, Lauren, there's a bit of a silver lining here. Take a couple of days off, I'll tell everyone you're under great stress because of your father, have a chat with Faye Sutton, and maybe I can get her to withdraw the complaint. Don't worry about things here. I'll arrange coverage. You go and take care of your dad."

***

Lauren drove up to her apartment and tensed at the sight of the beat-up Ford pickup truck parked in front. *Not now!* She was in no mood to face Chris, and she really could not spare the time for another argument. But her irritation eased when she saw her son standing on the lawn with her husband. Surely Chris would not have brought Joey along to witness the discord between his parents.

"Mommy!" Joey screamed when he recognized his mother's Volvo coming to a stop in the driveway.

Lauren stepped out and Joey hugged her around the waist. This was unusual, and Lauren, juggling her briefcase, gave him an awkward one-armed hug in return. "Hi, baby. How's my little man doing today?"

Joey had inherited his father's brown, curly hair and dark eyes, as well as his openness about feelings. "I miss you, Mommy," he answered, tightening his grip. "I want you to come home."

Lauren swallowed against a sudden tightening in her throat. "I miss you, too."

"Hello, Lauren," Chris said.

"If this is about the letter I received today, I have to tell you, your timing is terrible," she answered, straightening up. "And I really cannot talk about it right now."

"I am sorry about that, Lauren, but I've been leaving you messages on your phone all this week for you to call me. I wanted to tell you before they delivered it. And, of course, if I'd known about your father, I wouldn't have let them send it."

"You know?" Lauren blurted.

"Your mother called and told me. I am so sorry, Lauren." His face was sad, and Lauren knew his emotion was genuine. Chris and her father had got along well together. "How is he?"

"He had a large stroke that left him in a coma. That's not a good sign," she said solemnly. "I'm just going in to pack a bag, and then I'm going to catch the first plane to Philadelphia."

"Why don't we drive?" Chris said. When she stared blankly at him, he continued. "We're coming too. That's why we're here. We're all packed. I called the school and told them Joey won't be in for the rest of the week."

When did Chris become so assertive? Lauren wondered. "No. You stay here. I'm not even sure what's going on yet. I'll fly out, check out how my dad's doing. I might transfer him up here so he can get better care than that rinky-dink hospital in Hope."

"Lauren, your dad needs all the support he can get right now. So does your mom."

"Which is why I am going. But Joey needs to stay in school."

"He's in first grade, Lauren. I don't think missing a few days will affect his SAT scores," Chris replied in a tight voice. "And if things are bad, Joey has a right to be there. You may not think much of your father, but Joey loves him . . . and so do I."

"You don't know a damned thing about my father and me, Chris," she hissed. Joey stepped away, looking distraught by his mother's tone. His joy quickly soured.

"Honey, go into the apartment. You can watch TV while Dad and I talk a little. I'll be right in."

Joey looked at Chris, who said quietly, "Yes, Joey, go inside. We'll be in in a minute." The little boy looked doubtful, but took the keys and obediently went inside. Chris turned back to Lauren.

"Joey knows his grandfather is sick. He wants to see him."

"He doesn't know what a stroke means. I don't want him to see his beloved grandfather unconscious in a cold ICU room with tubes sticking out of him."

"You don't know Joey the way I do, Lauren. He's more mature than you give him credit for. He'll deal with it if he can just sit with his grandfather."

"Don't you *dare* lecture me about not knowing my own son," Lauren flared.

"Well, what do you expect? You're never around. What kind of relationship do you have with him when you're at the hospital all hours of the day, night and weekend? Admit it, you weren't surprised when he asked to stay with me when we separated."

"I give Joey everything he wants and needs," she protested, knowing it wasn't true.

"Except your time," Chris interjected. "How many T-ball games did you go to this year? I'll tell you—*none*. When was the last time you went to a conference at school? Oh, let me think, how about *never*? You give him toys and books and money, but you don't spend time with him. He needs that, Lauren. Just like I do."

Lauren nodded. "Oh, I see. This isn't about Joey's needs, it's about you. How many times do we have to go through this? You know that I have to do clinic, research, and hospital work as well as teaching if I'm to keep my position at Mass Gen."

Chris shook his head. "Is that all that matters? Even if it means neglecting your family, our son? Can't you see what your ambition is doing to us?"

"It's not ambition; it's responsibility. Patients depend on me and my work. As for what I'm 'doing to' Joey, I'm setting a good example for him to follow." *Not like his father*, Lauren almost added, but managed to choke back the words.

Chris seemed to sense the thought anyway. "Oh yes, I know how you justify it to yourself. But at the end of the day, it's all the same. You're never here for us. Well, have it your way, as usual," he said, turning away from her. "I'll be waiting inside the truck. I'll leave it to you to explain to Joey why you won't let him see his grandfather."

Lauren stared after him. Once, Chris had understood that medicine was her calling. He'd known the kind of person she was and loved her for it. *I'll be damned if I'm going to throw away all I worked for because my husband has suddenly decided out of the blue that I spend too much time away from home,* she thought.

As she approached the apartment, Lauren looked through the window beside the front door and saw Joey. He was sitting on the couch—just sitting, not playing with the toys in the box sitting in the living room beside the fireplace, not watching TV or reading a book. *What's he thinking? What's he feeling?* He looked so sad, just like in her screensaver picture.

Lauren sat on the couch next to her son.

"Baby, can I get you something?"

Joey shrugged. "I'm not a baby," he muttered.

Lauren sighed and patted him on the shoulder. "No. You're growing up, aren't you?" She put her arm around him. "I know you're sad about Poppy. I'm going to see him now, and I'm going to try to bring him back to Boston and make him better."

Joey stirred. "What if you can't? Can I go see him in Hope?"

"We'll see how it goes, okay?" Lauren said. Joey shot her a glance, then pulled away from her and bolted out of the apartment. Looking out the window, Lauren saw him run to the pickup and get in. The truck moved away. Lauren raised her hand to wave, but Joey never turned to look back at her.

Suddenly Lauren remembered sitting alone in her bedroom as a child, looking out the window as her mother said goodbye to her father, who was leaving once more for some mysterious assignment for the Army that would keep him away from them for months. Usually Lauren would be out there hugging him goodbye too, but this time, she remembered, she'd been angry with him for going and refused to acknowledge him when he left. When he'd looked up at her window and waved, she turned away.

CHAPTER SIX

LAUREN STARED OUT THE window of the small commuter plane as the last rays of sunset touched the tops of the mountains in southeastern Pennsylvania. She thought about the coal mines that had once been the livelihood for much of the population in the area. Most of the mines were now closed and, as a result, many families had moved to find work. Lauren recalled how her father lamented the damage caused to the scenic terrain by the old strip-mining techniques. He would reassure her during drives through the mountains that nature always reclaimed its own, pointing out places where trees were growing back.

Dad was right, Lauren thought, looking over the lush landscape below. *Nature is a powerful force.*

It had been two decades since she'd left the family home, and she had been back only a half a dozen times, and always at the insistence of others. She didn't see the point of staying in a dying town. She tried a number of times to get her parents to move to Boston near her, but they wouldn't even entertain the idea.

"Our life is here, Lauren. All of our friends are here. Our memories of you are here," her father would explain.

"Memories of me as a teenager? That's not who I am anymore, Dad. And you could make new memories in Boston," she persisted. "There's so much to *do* there. Plus, Dad, it has beautiful gardens. You'd love it."

"This is our home. It's who we are. We don't want to leave," he would say in his and-that's-final voice she remembered from childhood.

Hope held no appeal for her, and she visited as little as possible. If it wasn't for Joey wanting to see Poppy and Nana, she would happily have avoided going back at all.

As she drove the rented Prius from the airport across town to the hospital, she scanned the area thinking, *Nope, nothing's changed.* Her old high school still stood on Turner Avenue, looking weathered and depressed like the town it served. *Not many happy memories inside those walls,* she thought.

Although she enjoyed many of her high school classes, Lauren had not fit in with the other students and had few friends. She was a bookish introvert and rarely seen at a weekend party. Worse, she was never truly challenged academically. Of all of her accomplishments in life thus far, she would not count being the 1991 valedictorian of Hope Regional High School as one of her more difficult undertakings.

Her father moved the family from Northern Virginia when Lauren was thirteen. It was one in a string of moves, which made it hard for Lauren to make or keep friends. Moving to Hope had been the hardest. It was a backwater compared to bustling Northern Virginia and the cultural mecca of Washington DC, with its vast museums and libraries. Even though the damp climate and city smog aggravated her asthma, Lauren felt exhilarated there.

By contrast, the one-horse town of Hope, where they occasionally went to visit her grandmother until her death, offered nothing that interested Lauren. She was delighted when her parents informed her that her father was retiring from the military, but her delight turned to dismay when Joe Keller announced the family would be moving into the old family home in Hope.

"But all of my friends are here," Lauren had lied.

"The weather here in the DC area is not the best for your asthma, Lauren. You know that. You don't want to be hospitalized for it again," Joe Keller said.

"Like it'll be much different in Hope?" she snapped.

"Actually, the doctors here did recommend a different climate, one similar to Hope."

"I don't care. There's nothing to do in Hope. How am I going to get into Harvard going to a small, rural high school? Don't do this to me, Dad. Please?" she begged.

"Honey, opportunity is where you make it. With your grades, your tests scores and your natural smarts and ability, you'll excel at anything you do, wherever you end up," her father replied gently, sitting next to her on her bed.

"No!" she screamed, standing and walking to the window. "Hope was *your* home, not mine. And you didn't go to college. I don't want to end up like you."

As soon as the words left her lips, Lauren regretted them. She thought about taking them back, but as she turned back to face her father, he was already walking towards her bedroom door.

"I'm sorry you feel that way, Lauren. But know that your health is the most important thing to me. You may not understand this now, but hopefully, someday you will."

Once again, Joe had been right. After their move to Hope, Lauren graduated first in her high school class and did go on to Harvard. Although she never admitted it to her father, she grew to understand the decisions made that day. But back then, moving to Hope had been difficult for the awkward teenager, struggling to find her identity after so many military moves. Making matters worse was that her father became a gardener, of all things, a profession that held no interest for his daughter, who had no desire to spend her spare time digging in the dirt.

Even though he hadn't gone to college, Lauren always thought her father a special man, taking pride that he was important enough to travel the world for the Army. That helped her justify his long absences. Now, he was a blue-collar laborer, a commoner no better than the men who worked the failing mines of central Pennsylvania. So, Lauren did what she always had—isolated herself and escaped into her books.

Her 4.0 GPA and academic awards came easy as she lacked the typical distractions of teenaged life. She had one goal—to graduate and leave that dump of a town.

Her parents said they were proud of her, but she saw the pain in their eyes at losing her when she left for Boston. They knew she wouldn't be coming back. That was okay with her; she was the one leaving for the world, to make something of herself, while they were the ones laboring in a backwater town.

Joey's decision to live with his father instead of her made Lauren appreciate how her parents must have felt when she left them. As she drove, she grew angry that they refused to leave. Had they been in Boston, her father would likely have been recovered by now instead of in a coma because he lay in the dirt for six hours. *Perhaps now my mother will listen*, Lauren thought.

"One day," she said aloud. "That's all I need here."

The route to the hospital crossed Rockwell Avenue, and on impulse she turned right and drove two blocks north, stopping in front of her parents' house. The narrow two-story house was modest even by Hope standards. It was painted an immaculate white, with crimson shutters and a large front porch. Although the yard was small, it was landscaped beautifully, no doubt the envy of everyone on the street. The house as well was beautifully kept as it always had been, Lauren recalled with a smile. Her father worked on that old house every free moment he had.

Joe Keller had been raised in that house, as had his mother before him. Lauren had fond memories of Grammy Keller. She was warm and sweet, the kind of grandmother who always seemed to be just taking a fresh batch of cookies out of the oven. But there was a touch of sadness in her, no doubt linked to an unspoken mystery about her husband, Lauren's grandfather. Lauren had never known him and had been told nothing more than that he died and that it would upset Grammy too much to talk about him.

Her own father never mentioned him. Neither did Uncle Harry.

Lauren remembered one visit a couple of years before her grandmother died. Her father, home on leave from the military, had decided to replace the old coal furnace in his mother's house and asked Lauren for some help while her mother and grandmother were out shopping. Lauren was eleven at the time and felt proud that her father treated her as if she was as strong and capable as a boy. But she was equally annoyed because she wanted to peruse her grandmother's set of encyclopedias—not spend the afternoon in the damp basement of her grandmother's old house helping her father rip out a dirty coal bin. Still, she went, reluctantly heeding his admonition to use her inhaler first so the mildew wouldn't trigger her asthma.

That day ended up being one of the fondest memories she had of her dad. Usually he was the strong, silent type, but being down in the basement put him in a chatty mood, and for once he talked about his childhood.

"Your uncle Harry and I would come down here to play hide and seek when we were your age, Rennie," he told her. "I would pretend to look for him while he hid right over there under those steps. Other days, we'd play down here for hours, pretending this was a submarine and we were the captains. Harry always wanted to be the boss captain, but, more often than not, he would get our sub sunk by the Germans."

She listened as he told story after story of growing up on 205 Rockwell Avenue and wondered how her own life might have been different had she had a sibling. Being an only child was a lonely existence, especially when you were uncomfortable around new people. But she also noted how her father had spent his childhood in an imaginary world with his kid brother. Lauren had never enjoyed playing make believe; even as a child she preferred reading textbooks, science magazine articles, encyclopedias—anything that contained facts and data about the real world.

Still, that moment in the basement was a rare happy time for both of them. She couldn't think of a similar moment. She recalled the time he made the mistake of calling her by his pet nickname, *Rennie,* in front of Josh Harvith. Lauren had had a crush on Josh since the first day of high school. One day when she was coming out of a store in what passed for Hope's downtown, she encountered Josh, who actually stopped to talk to her. But her delight was cut short when her dad drove by, honked the horn of his ancient pickup, and yelled, "Hi, Rennie!"

Josh laughed and walked off. Lauren wasn't sure if the boy was laughing at her nickname or her father's beat-up old pickup truck, but either way Lauren was mortified. That night she created a scene at home and made her father promise never again to honk at her or call her that childish nickname. He kept his word, as he always did, and never uttered the name Rennie again.

***

Lauren felt a wave of sadness staring at the old house. Pushing the emotion away, she put the car in gear, turned left at the next block, and returned to Main Street, which would take her to the hospital. *If you can even call it that,* she thought as she turned into the parking lot a few minutes later. It was hardly larger than a clinic; the old building was too small to house even one department of Mass General.

A single door led into the hospital from the visitor parking lot. No electronic or rotating doors here, only a large, ornate, heavy wooden door with brass handles, probably dating from the ribbon-cutting fifty years ago. Very little inside the unadorned foyer had changed since her last visit here in high school. Corridors with tiled floors led off in three directions from the empty reception area littered with a few old and worn but comfortable-looking couches and chairs.

She glanced at the pictures of the hospital administrators on one wall, all white males in their fifties or sixties. *So much for progress in Hope, Pennsylvania.* Then she focused on one familiar face, that of the man she now had to confront to get her father transferred to Mass General. She knew she was going to be in for a fight, but she was confident she would win against country doctor Douglas Spiva.

The ICU was down the hall to the left. As she started down it, a door opened and a man stepped out. Lauren's heart lifted. He was of average height and stocky. Although only in his early sixties, his receding hairline and gray hair made him look much older, but his eyes revealed a sharp intelligence. He saw her, immediately smiled and approached.

"Lauren!"

"Hi, Uncle Harry," Lauren said, returning his smile as he pulled her into a hug.

Lauren was very fond of her uncle. Like her, Harry had left this town and made something of himself, gone to law school and become a successful attorney. But like his brother, he chose to return to Hope, which baffled Lauren. He had been near the top of his class at Georgetown Law School and could have written his ticket in Philadelphia, New York, or any other big city in the Northeast. When Harry came to Lauren's medical school graduation in Boston, she asked him why he had stayed in Hope.

"You could do so much better in a larger city," she told him, speaking as one professional to another.

"My dear, people are the same everywhere you go. People in small towns have problems just as important to them as the people in the big cities. They need help, too, Lauren. I grew up in Hope. Hope is my home; those are my people. If I can help them, I will."

He sounded like her father. Lauren was baffled by the hold Hope, Pennsylvania, seemed to have on the Keller brothers.

Well, at least Uncle Harry got out and got an education, unlike Dad.

"Good to see you," Harry said as he released her from the hug. "I'm so glad you're here. It means so much to your mom that you've come. She's taking this very hard, you know," he said sadly.

"Where is she?" Lauren asked. "Is she in Dad's room?"

"She just left," Harry answered. "She's been here all day. I only got her to go home by telling her I'd wait here for you. She'll be back in a couple of hours, unless we call to say something's changed before then."

"How *is* Dad?" she asked as they walked down the hall together.

"Doug says it's pretty bad. He's had a major stroke and has been in a coma since they found him." Harry went on to tell Lauren the circumstances of how and when Joe had been found.

"Mom told me. They found him in the dirt in some lady's garden. She said he could have been there for six hours or more." Lauren tried to compose herself but grew angry. "He shouldn't be lifting heavy bushes or digging holes at his age. He should have retired years ago," she said, forcefully. "I've told him again and again he should be taking it easy."

"When has your father ever taken it easy?" Harry replied with a wry smile. "Gardening is what he loves to do. What if someone told you that you should stop practicing medicine?" The smile faded. Harry's voice trembled as he said, "I still can't believe it. Joe's always been the strong one. It seems so wrong that I have to look after him, when he's always been the one to watch over me."

"What do you mean?" Lauren asked, puzzled. She'd never seen Harry lean on her father for anything; she always thought of Uncle Harry as tough and independent. Her role model seemed to grow frail right in front of her eyes.

"I'll tell you later. Now that you are here, I'm going to grab something to eat. I'll be back soon." He embraced her again and turned toward the outer door. Lauren's attention switched to the task at hand.

***

The ICU was, like the hospital, small and modest. It had just five beds fanning out like rays from a star, which was the nurses' station. There was only one nurse behind the counter, going through a patient's chart. She looked far too young to be in charge of an ICU shift; in fact, she looked almost too young to have finished nursing school. Perhaps her supervisor was off getting coffee or in a patient's room. Lauren hoped so.

"I'm looking for Joseph Keller," Lauren announced abruptly.

The nurse looked up. "Ma'am, I'm sorry, family visiting hours are over. You'll have to come back tomorrow," she said politely.

A quick glance at the name on the binding of the chart she was holding told Lauren that the chart was her father's and that he was in bed number three. Heads would have rolled at her hospital if anyone ever wrote down a patient's name on the outside of a chart, which was forbidden in order to prevent precisely what Lauren had just done—ascertain the location of her father without even asking.

"Joe Keller is my father, and I'm not simply family. I'm Dr. Lauren Keller from Massachusetts General in Boston, and I would like to review the chart notes and films," Lauren stated confidently, demanding, not asking.

The nurse's eyes grew wide. "Um, I don't think—"

Lauren interrupted her. "Is that room three?" she asked, pointing to the third point on the star.

"Yes, ma'am, but—" the nurse began. Lauren ignored her and stepped toward the curtain-covered sliding glass doors that opened into ICU. As she approached, she heard a man talking inside. Lauren glanced over her shoulder to the nurse, who was staring at her.

"I thought you said visiting hours were over?" she huffed.

"Um, Dr. Spiva, Mr. Keller's doctor, is in there right now. I don't know who that other man is, but he came in with Dr. Spiva."

Lauren turned and opened the sliding door. Her glance took in the figure in the bed first, then passed to the man standing next to her father.

Dr. Douglas Spiva had aged considerably since she'd last seen him but still looked like the country doctor he had always been. Beside him was a tall, imposing man, a stranger to Lauren.

"Lauren," Doug Spiva exclaimed with a grand smile. "I'm glad you're here. It's been a long time. It's so good to see you again, although I wish it were under better circumstances," he went on, lowering his glasses to rest low on the bridge of his nose and looking at her over them. "Did you see your uncle outside? Your mother's just gone home."

"Hello, Doctor," Lauren replied. "Yes, I saw Uncle Harry." She looked at the stranger, noticing the tattoo on one large, muscular forearm, a tattoo she had seen many times before—a simple yellow triangle superimposed on a green sword. "You served with my father," she said, looking up at him.

"Yes, Lauren. We've met before, when you were very young," the big man replied.

"I'm afraid I don't remember," Lauren said, looking away from him to her father.

Taking the hint the man said, "And you're here to see your father, so I'll get out of the way. Well, Doc," the stranger said to Dr. Spiva, "thank you again for everything. I'll see you tomorrow." As he walked past Lauren on his way out, he put a strong but gentle hand on her shoulder. "I'm glad you came home. We'll talk tomorrow." He opened the door and left.

"Who was that?" Lauren asked Dr. Spiva.

"I've met him once or twice before at your parents' house. His name's Mike. Come to think of it, I don't think I ever caught his last name. He's obviously very close to your father," the doctor replied. "Very concerned about his friend."

"How *is* Dad?" Lauren asked, knowing the answer. She had seen enough patients in ICU beds to read the signs. Her father had EKG leads attached to his chest to monitor his heart, intravenous tubes in both arms, and an arterial line in his right wrist. Such tubes allowed easy and fast administration of needed medicines as well as a mixture of nutrients to keep his body going. All of his vital signs were being fed into a monitor on the wall above the head of the bed, beeping in time with her father's slow but regular heartbeat. Her father was also intubated; a tube had been put down his throat, and a large, rather antiquated (to Lauren's eyes) ventilator next to the bed was noisily breathing for him. All of this added up to one fact—he was on full life support.

Lauren was glad she had been firm with Chris back in Boston and hadn't allowed Joey to come see his grandfather this way. As a physician, she was accustomed to these scenes, but it was still hard even for her to look at someone she loved in this condition. The scene would have devasted her son.

"Let's step outside," Dr. Spiva suggested in his warm voice, leading Lauren through the sliding door back to the nurses' station. "It doesn't look good, Lauren. Joe suffered a right middle cerebral artery infarct. He's since developed some intracranial swelling. He hasn't regained consciousness since being brought in."

"Has he had thrombolytics?" Lauren asked, referring to medicine that could dissolve a clot, the usual cause of a stroke.

"No. We really didn't know how long he was down on the lawn before Mrs. Boudreaux found him, but it was well over six hours. By the time he got to the emergency room, it was too late. You know the protocol."

"Of course, I do," Lauren said, trying not to sound shrill. She didn't need some country doctor telling her the rules for stroke treatment, which dictated that thrombolytics to dissolve a clot could only be given in the first few hours after a stroke occurred. Over Dr. Spiva's shoulder, she noticed the young nurse listening in on their conversation. Lauren glared at her; the nurse dropped her eyes to her computer screen.

"Believe me, all that could have been done for your father has been done. He's on antiplatelet therapy, now," Dr. Spiva said.

Lauren was not convinced. "I'd like to see his chart and films. In the morning I'm calling Dr. Hans Jurgesson. He's been doing some great work on endovascular therapy and intracranial stenting up at Mass General. In fact, I want to transfer Dad there tomorrow," she said. "I'll start arranging for a bed for him up there today."

"Lauren. Your father's staying here," Dr. Spiva replied softly, taking off his glasses and looking squarely at her. Despite his gentle manner, his eyes were unyielding. "I've known your father a long time, and we had several discussions about end-of-life situations before filling out his advanced directive form. Your father's wishes were very clear. He would not want extraordinary measures at this point."

"You may call them *extraordinary measures* here, but they're *standard treatment* where I work," Lauren shot back. *If only I'd been the one to talk with Dad about his options instead of Dr. We're-Doing-The-Best-We-Can*, she thought bitterly. *I should have foreseen this.* "As his daughter and a physician, I disagree with your interpretation of his wishes. I want him transferred."

Dr. Spiva sighed. "It's not up to you, Lauren. Your mother has the medical power of attorney. She has told me to respect Joe's wishes. Legally that binds me—and you too."

"He'll die here and you know it!" Lauren shouted. The nurse stopped pretending to type and stared at her.

"Lauren, I'm sorry, but his prognosis is poor no matter what we might try now."

She noticed Dr. Spiva's sympathetic eyes. She knew what he was thinking, that her emotions over her father's grave condition clouded what she knew, as a physician, was reality. That it was too late for any treatment to help her father and she was not yet ready to accept that she was going to lose him.

"Look at his films," he continued, pointing to the images of Joe's brain that hung on the lighted radiology box on the wall next to his room.

Lauren felt a chill run through her as she examined the radiographic films of her father's brain. She wasn't a radiologist but had seen enough films to know there was extensive temporal and middle lobe damage clearly evident on the scans. But she also wasn't a neurosurgeon or neuroradiologist. Perhaps Hans could see hope where she saw only a grim outcome.

"I'd still like to send these films up to Dr. Jurgesson for his opinion," she said.

Dr. Spiva considered the request, then nodded. "Well, it can't hurt," he ceded. "Go ahead and have the files sent to Dr. Jurgesson. But Lauren, you're not his physician. I am. And my advice is for you to just be with your father now," he said. "As his *daughter.* That's what he needs most." He nodded and walked out of the ICU.

Lauren stood looking after him. She felt cold and alone. It wasn't like her to feel so helpless. She was always the one in control, always the one that made things happen. And it was her job to heal people. She might have been estranged from Joe, but he was still her father and she did love him. *There has to be a way,* she thought as she slowly walked into the room and looked down at Joe. He seemed shrunken as he lay without moving, so unlike the man she knew. Her determination strengthened. If Hans replied that there may be a way to save her father, then she would transfer him despite Dr. Spiva's orders. All she had to do was convince her mother to agree.

***

"Hey again," said her uncle Harry, walking into his brother's ICU room with a white bag that he undoubtedly received from the small hospital cafeteria. "I got you a burger, too, in case you haven't eaten."

"Oh, I'm—" Lauren was going to say she wasn't hungry, but the smell of the burger was enticing. "Sure," she conceded.

Harry handed her a warm, wrapped burger and some napkins. Lauren took it and sat in the chair near her father. "I saw Doug on his way out. How are you doing?" he asked.

"I haven't given up hope," Lauren answered between bites. "Dr. Spiva's agreed to a second opinion, did he tell you?"

"Yep. Anything that could save Joe sounds like a good idea to me." He regarded his niece thoughtfully. "You must be exhausted."

"No, I'm fine," Lauren murmured. She looked up at him. "What did you mean when you said Dad always took care of you? Do you mean when you were kids? Dad told me stories about how you'd play hide and seek in the basement."

Harry looked down at his brother, his eyes warm but sad.

"Yeah, we spent a lot of time hiding down there." His gaze moved to Lauren. "Did he ever talk about our father, your grandfather? About how things were for us as kids?"

Lauren shrugged. "No, he didn't. I know your father died at a relatively young age. And that there wasn't much money after that. Dad didn't say, but I always guessed that's why he went in the Army so young." She looked at her uncle. "I've always wondered about my grandfather."

Harry sat on the foot of Joe's bed. "Well. I'll start by telling you that I wasn't always the person I am now. When I was a kid, I was very self-conscious. You see, I had a bad speech problem. I stuttered horribly."

"Really?" Lauren knew that childhood conditions like a stammer could be overcome with the right kind of intervention, but Harry Keller had managed to do even more than that; he was an elegant, persuasive, and powerful speaker. In high school, Lauren would stop by the courthouse on her way home from school just to watch her uncle Harry argue cases. There wasn't a lawyer in the county that could beat her uncle when it came to presenting a case to a jury. She'd been so impressed, in fact, that she toyed with the idea of becoming a lawyer. In the end, however, her love of science and her desire to heal people won out.

"Do you know why I overcame my speech impediment?" he asked, allowing a small smile.

"To become a successful lawyer?" Lauren guessed.

"No, I wanted to be more like my brother," replied Harry. "I wanted to be the kind of man he was. Still is, to me," he added sadly, looking at Joe.

"What do you mean? You worked your way through college and law school and have a successful career as a lawyer. Dad never had that kind of ambition. He never went to college. He spent twenty years in the Army and then became a landscaper," Lauren countered. "I don't see how he was a role model for you."

"I know you can't see it," Harry replied, nodding sadly. "To understand it, you'd have to know more about your father. And your grandfather. Quite frankly, it's a good thing that you didn't know him."

"When did he die? And how?" Lauren asked.

"Oh, years before you were born. He was found in an alley in Pittsburgh. They don't know if the drink or the freezing cold got to him first. He was an angry and bitter man, our father. Worse, he was an alcoholic. I don't think I ever saw him completely sober. Every night that man would drink. The more he drank, the more abusive he became. He teased me mercilessly when I would stutter. It only made me more nervous around him, which made me stutter more. He used to call me Harriett when he would drink. 'Harriett, my sickly little girl,'" Harry recalled. Lauren winced at the pain on her uncle's face.

"Your father used to take me into the basement or upstairs to play games with me when Dad was drinking. After a while, I realized he was letting me win those games so I would cheer up, feel better about myself, have more confidence. I loved him for that." Harry smiled. "He was more of a father to me than your grandfather ever was. He was gregarious and outgoing as a child. Very confident and sure of himself. It was infectious. At school, everyone wanted to be Joe's friend. I was so proud of him. Proud to be his brother. People at school talked to me because they were Joe's friends or wanted to be his friend.

"Then it all changed. I remember it like it was yesterday. It was a cold December night in 1966," Harry continued, shivering despite the warmth of the room. "Dad was in a particularly foul mood that night. As usual, he'd been in a tavern drinking before he came home, and he kept on drinking . . ."

CHAPTER SEVEN

December 1966, Hope, Pennsylvania

"C-CAH-COACH RYDZY WAS IN a *ba-bad* mood tonight," Harry told his big brother as they walked down Main Street through the dark, cold night. The wind had died down and all was quiet on the snowy streets of Hope. Harry appreciated the night stillness. He was in no rush to get home, where things were rarely calm.

"But you did good, Harry. Twenty-two points! If the others had played as well as you, Coach wouldn't have been so mad," Joe said, putting his gloved hand on the younger boy's shoulder.

"Johnny *d-di-did* well. All those rebounds he c-caught. Coach shouldn't have b-benched him like that. We would've *wa-wa-won*."

"Just because you're a star player on the team, doesn't mean you can intentionally foul someone like Johnny did. Coach was right for benching him, even if you lost the game because of it. He was teaching all of you a life lesson that's more important than the game," Joe said as they turned the corner onto Rockwell Avenue.

"I *ga-guess*. But it sure would have been n-n-nice to win."

"The team's getting better with each game, Harry, don't worry. Just keep doing your part," Joe reassured him. He had just turned seventeen and seemed more like a father than big brother.

Harry nodded, looking at the narrow house they were approaching. The white paint was cracking, the shutters needed fixing, and the yard was as bleak as the soul of its owner. Most of the lights were on, which meant their father was home. If their mother had been alone, only the porch and kitchen lights would be on. The porch lights would welcome her sons home from the game, and Isabella usually spent most of her time in the kitchen, which their father considered "women's territory."

Harry stopped at the driveway as he heard the raised voices coming from the living room. *It's happening more often*, he thought as he looked down at the freshly fallen snow, praying that yelling and screaming would be the worst thing that happened tonight.

"Harry," Joe said quietly as he led his younger brother to the door. "Go right upstairs when we go in, okay?"

"*O-o-k-kay*," Harry replied.

Joe turned the knob as quietly as he could, even as the shouts inside grew louder. The door opened wide enough for the two brothers to slip inside. Fortunately, the foyer light was off, and they crept up the staircase without being noticed. Before he went up, Joe flipped off the porch light, letting their mother know they were home and waiting upstairs until the fireworks died down.

Safe inside their upstairs bedroom, Harry sat on the bottom bunk bed. *It's wrong that we have to be afraid inside our own house*, he thought. Then he jumped at the sound of something breaking.

Joe opened the door. "I'm going downstairs to make sure Mom's okay. You stay here," he said and, without looking back, left the room.

Harry sat alone, listening to the incoherent yells coming from downstairs. After a few minutes he opened his book bag and took out his math book, hoping to divert his thoughts. However, he couldn't focus and soon slammed the book shut. The wall clock showed it was ten minutes past their usual dinnertime.

Steps sounded on the stairs and the door swung open wide. "It's just me. Let's go. Dinner's late and he's mad as hell about it.

Be careful—he'll fly off the handle at just about anything tonight," Joe warned.

The brothers went into the dining room. Frank Keller was sitting and waiting. He stared glassy-eyed at them as they took their seats, but said nothing. Their mother, Isabella, put full plates in front of them with a look of warning. Frank began cutting his pork chop with unsteady hands as Isabella returned from the kitchen with her own plate and sat.

The boys ate as quietly and as quickly as they could, wanting only to get back to their upstairs bedroom. Then it happened; as he reached for the salt, Harry's arm brushed his glass and milk spilled across the table. The two teenagers and their mother froze, waiting for Frank's reaction.

"What the hell's a matter with you, boy? For chrissake; stupid klutz!" he bellowed.

"I'm *s-so-sorry, Da-dad*. I'll *cl-clean* it up," Harry said, jumping up from his seat to reach for the napkins on the table.

"Let your mother do that," Frank blared. "That's women's work. When are you going to *m-ma-ma man* up and stop being such a *gi-gi-girl*?" he mocked.

Joe deliberately rose and started sopping up the milk with his napkin. Harry stared at him. It had always been Joe's policy not to provoke their father, but the older boy said, "Stop picking on Harry. It was just an accident."

Joe didn't get to finish his sentence. Frank whipped his hand across his oldest son's mouth. Isabella shrieked as Joe crashed to the floor. She flew to his side and wiped at the blood trickling down from the corner of his mouth.

"That was an accident, too," Frank said, and began to laugh. He leaned in his chair and looked down at Joe bleeding on the floor. "I'm picking on you, now, instead. Happy?"

"Why did you have to go and do that?" Isabella moaned as Joe stood.

"He'll learn to mind his own business one way or another," Frank roared, shoving another piece of pork chop into his mouth and washing it down with a big gulp of beer.

"I'm fine, Mom," Joe said, giving her a small smile and sitting back down in his chair.

"See? Stop whining, Isabella. At least the boy isn't a sissy like *Ha-Ha* Harry*ett* over there. So, don't treat him like one," Frank slurred.

Not another word was spoken at dinner. As soon as Frank made his unsteady way into the living room, the boys began to clear the dishes. Joe washed while Harry quietly dried the dirty plates. The television came on, but over it they could hear Frank grumbling away at their mother.

"Thanks for sticking up for *m-me*, Joe," said Harry. "I'm *s-s-sorry* he *h-hit* you."

Joe didn't answer. He turned toward the living room as Frank's voice grew louder.

"*W-what* is it, *J-Joe*?" asked Harry, seeing the concern on his brother's face.

Just then they heard a crash in the other room. Startled, Harry dropped the glass he was drying. Joe was already running out of the kitchen. When he caught up to Joe at the entrance to the living room, Harry saw their mother on the floor, bleeding from her disfigured nose. A broken vase lay beside her. Frank was standing over her with clenched fists, cursing.

Joe leapt on his father. Frank Keller was a big man, over six feet tall, 220 pounds of blue-collar muscle. Joe was fifty pounds lighter, but he was propelled by a surge of adrenaline from the sight of his hurt mother and the element of surprise. He grabbed his father and threw him up against the wall and then helped Isabella up from the floor and out of the room.

Enraged, Frank went after his eldest son. But he was so drunk Joe easily ducked his swings and then with a stiff jab connected with Frank's chin. Their father staggered back and fell heavily to the floor.

He lay still as Joe stood over him.

"You will never lay a hand on any of us again," Joe said to him in a quiet, intense voice. "Do you understand? Never again."

Frank slowly rose and looked at his family lined up against him across the room. Then he turned, took his coat from off the hook in the foyer and staggered out the door.

***

"We never saw Dad again," Harry told his niece. "The neighbors had heard Mom's screams and called the police, who showed up soon after Dad left. They called for an ambulance to take Mom to the hospital. Later they looked for Dad, but they didn't find him. We didn't hear anything about him until he was found dead in Pittsburgh several years later."

"I've never seen my dad lose his temper," Lauren mused, picturing in her mind the scene in the living room.

"He didn't, even then. Joe told me he saw something in our father's eyes that night. He knew he had to act or something even worse would happen to Mom or to me. That's the night Joe grew up, stopped being a kid. But I'm not sure he'd ever really been allowed to be a kid, not like the way he tried to let me still have some semblance of a childhood for as long as possible. I'd never realized just how badly our dad abused Mom. They both hid it from me. Joe later said to me that he was only ten years old when he realized he had to be the man of the house and help take care of me and Mom."

"Why didn't Grandma leave? Why did she put up with the abuse?"

"Oh, you know, Lauren, that generation stuck things out even when they were bad. Divorces weren't very popular back then. Besides, she had us to think about. She had no job skills. How could she look after us?"

"Well, how *did* she take care of you guys after your father left?"

"She started watching babies and toddlers in our home. Everyone knew your grandmother; after Dad was out of the picture, many parents dropped off their kids for her to watch. Joe worked on weekends and a few nights a week at the local hardware store, and I did odd jobs around town." He glanced at Lauren. "Did you know he was accepted to Penn State?" Lauren looked up, face flush with bewilderment. "I'll take that surprised look on your face as a no. He was going to study engineering. Mom was so proud. Her son, the engineer."

"But he didn't go to college."

"That's right, he didn't," Harry replied softly. "Because of Mom and me. There just wasn't enough money. College, as you know, is expensive. So is a mortgage, doctors' bills, food and utilities. Joe knew that what little money we had would quickly be used up on his college tuition, leaving little, if any, for us to live on. Times were lean back then. When Joe turned eighteen, there weren't a lot of employment prospects for someone without a trade. The Army offered training, benefits and a steady paycheck that would go a long way in Hope, Pennsylvania. Joe talked it over with me. He knew he'd get sent to Vietnam, but that didn't scare him. If anything, he joked that he'd have nothing to spend his money on in the jungle, so he could send more of it home to me and Mom. And I've always suspected that the routine and the rules of the military appealed to him, especially after the chaos that had been our home life."

Lauren nodded. That part made sense. "But why did he stay in? He could have left the service after two years and gone to college on the GI Bill. I know some residents that have done that."

"You're right," Harry said. "And in fact, he almost did get out and go to college when he first got back from Vietnam. It's my fault that he didn't."

"*Your* fault?" Lauren repeated.

"Afraid so. You see, I admired my big brother so much. Still do," Harry added softly, looking at Joe's still face in the bed. "But I wanted to be my own man. I needed to be independent, to prove myself. When I graduated from high school, Joe told me over and over to go to college, but I didn't listen. He said he'd sent enough money home for me to go. They'd instituted a draft lottery by then, and my number was high, so it wasn't likely I'd be called up, but I enlisted anyway. I didn't really think about the danger. After all, Joe had made it through his first tour in Vietnam without a scratch. But by the late '60s things were heating up over there more than I realized, despite the news. Joe knew this more than anyone."

Harry shook his head. "The day I joined, I was so proud. I wanted him to be proud of me as well. But when I told him, I saw a look of fear come over his face, then sadness. He told me I had no idea what I was getting into. Then he left, and the next I heard, he was back in Vietnam. I don't know how he did it, what strings he pulled, but when I got out of basic training, I was assigned to Joe's unit. You know, the Army doesn't usually let brothers serve together, but Joe always got what he went after. He was that determined to keep on watching over me, he gave up his own college dreams for me."

Lauren could only sit and watch the expression of love on her uncle's face. She remembered how her father would root for Penn State during football season. He had even mentioned the school to her when she was applying to colleges at the end of her high school years.

At the time, she thought his attachment to Penn was because Harry had gone there for his undergraduate degree. But now she realized that he'd wanted her to go to the school he never got to, for her to live out at least one dream for him. She remembered with a pang how she had loftily replied that she could do better. Her sights had always been on Harvard, or at the very least another Ivy League school. Penn State was not Ivy League, so she didn't even apply.

Harry went on, "I was naive. I didn't think about what Joe was sacrificing for me. I wasn't even mad that he felt he needed to keep an eye on me in Vietnam. I thought it was going to be fun having my big brother, my best friend, to hang around with in all those foreign ports. I had all these exotic dreams of traveling the world with Joe.

Like we used to play when we were kids. When I first got to Vietnam, I was full of excitement. Well, you can imagine how quickly my grand illusions were shattered."

He stood, went to the sink in the room, and poured some water into a paper cup. "And then, of course, there came the day when Joe saved my life." He returned and sat back down. "Have you ever heard that story?"

"No," Lauren answered. "Dad never told me anything about his Army life. I always thought that's because he was in special operations and couldn't." *And when I was a teenager, I wasn't interested*, she admitted to herself.

"This happened long before those days," Harry said. "Would you like to know just what kind of hero your father really is?" He looked closely at her. "It can wait, though, if you're tired. I know you've had a long day."

Lauren shook her head. "I'm used to long days," she told her uncle. "I want to hear your story."

CHAPTER EIGHT

October 1971, The Republic of Vietnam

THE 1ST BRIGADE OF the 101st Airborne Division began arriving in Vietnam in mid-1971. Although the majority of the unit was based on the southern coast, the Keller brothers' battalion was sent to the northernmost part of Quang Tri province, near the demilitarized zone. It was a difficult time to be in Vietnam. American forces had been learning the hard way how to fight a guerrilla war.

The men in Alpha Company had just arrived and were getting used to the austere environment of their new forward operating base, or FOB, which was little more than a hilltop cleared of all trees, surrounded by the curled-up barbed wire known as concertina wire. There were a number of medium and large tents scattered throughout the camp. An artillery company was due to join them the following month for some extra firepower to support the men on patrols, but, for now, Alpha Company was on its own.

Staff Sergeant Joseph Keller had been made platoon sergeant. He assigned Private Harold Keller to 1st Squad. On a particularly warm fall day, 1st Squad was relaxing in its tent, waiting for lunch to be served in the mess tent down the road. Most of the men were asleep on their cots. Joe was down at the battalion command post with the company commander.

Joe was not just an experienced soldier known for coolness under fire. He had a great sense of tactics, and the commander often called him into planning meetings to bounce ideas off of him.

While Joe was gone, another squad that had been out on patrol got pinned down right outside the base. Harry learned of the firefight after hearing mortar fire in the distance, a noise he had become accustomed to. Corporal Garcia, their squad leader, stormed into the tent.

"2nd Squad's getting hammered just outside the FOB. Mount up, girls," he shouted. Everyone in the squad looked at each other as the young corporal grabbed his rifle and some grenades off his bunk and ran out of the tent. They had been in-country for weeks, but had never gone on a mission without their platoon sergeant. They all admired Staff Sergeant Keller, but Corporal Garcia was considered a loose cannon.

"The hell with that," Big Dan Malone said. "I ain't goin' nowhere with him. Where's the sarge, anyway?"

"He's down the road at the command post with the captain," replied Rick Desimone, the radioman, who had not moved from his cot. The other men were also hanging back.

Harry knew that the chain of command, whether they liked it or not, put Corporal Garcia as their immediate supervisor. They had little choice but to follow the rogue corporal.

"Let's go, guys. 2nd Squad needs us," Harry said firmly, getting up from his cot and putting on his gear.

"But what about your bro, Harry? Why don't we wait for him? You know what Garcia's like. He'll get us killed out there," Malone protested.

"The men in 2nd *are* under attack. Joe would want us to help 'em."

The other men got up and followed Harry down to the makeshift front gate of the FOB, where Corporal Garcia was waiting, dancing with impatience.

"Alright, ladies. Let's go get some!" Garcia yelled. He ran out of the compound and down into the rice paddies that surrounded the base. The rest of the squad watched in horror as their squad leader charged recklessly through the killing fields in front of them.

"Garcia, wait!" Harry yelled, trying to slow down and take some cover. But Garcia ignored him and kept going. Harry swore and went after him. Reluctantly, the rest of the squad followed.

To everyone's relief, Garcia took a knee just at the edge of the vast jungle in front of him, about a quarter of a mile from the base. Harry was the first to reach his squad leader, panting from running as fast as he could through the muddy rice paddies.

"What's going on, exactly?" Harry asked as the squad rallied at the tree line. Garcia, his eyes wide open and looking crazed, stared out into the jungle in front of him as mortars hit closer and closer to their position.

"Garcia, come on!" Harry shouted, grabbing the corporal's arm and shaking it. "Tell us what we need to know!"

The corporal seemed to come out of his trance. "Bobby radioed that he was pinned down on the hilltop over by the river. That's all I know."

Harry looked around. The dense forest in front of them thinned out about 100 meters to their left. There, a small ravine cut through before the trees got thick again, going up the hill on the other side. He knew 2nd Squad had been sent that way to look for a tunnel the Viet Cong might be using to bring in mortars for shelling the FOB.

"Who's backing us up?" asked Harry.

"What?" Garcia asked. "Uh, I don't know. I was in the radio room and heard Bobby on the line calling for help, so I ran to get you guys."

"You mean no one knows we're here? No one told you to come out here? Are you crazy? What if the old man's calling in artillery on this position right now? You just can't run into a kill zone without telling someone. Damn you, Garcia!" Harry shouted. "Rick, call up to the battalion CP. Tell them to let Captain McFarley know what's going on."

"What about 2nd?" Big Dan asked, as the sounds of enemy machine guns in front of them intensified. Between the bursts, they could hear the faint screams of their comrades. All eight men in 1st Squad tensed. They had friends in 2nd Squad. Those could be the screams of someone they knew. A choice had to be made. Return to the FOB behind them, or forge ahead to help their friends before they were all slaughtered.

"We gotta go get 'em. If we can make it down to the ravine just to the south, we can come up on their rear. Hurry up, we don't have much time!" yelled Harry. Behind him he could hear Rick relaying the situation to the command post.

"Damn it, Harry, *I'm* in charge here. *I'm* the squad leader," Garcia snapped.

"Then be in charge, damn it! Take the lead. And try not to get us all killed."

Garcia looked at Harry with resentment. No one in the squad respected hot-headed Garcia. Sergeant Keller had raked the young corporal over the coals a number of times for poor judgment and had even tried to have Garcia relieved of duty on more than one occasion.

"I'll show you!" Garcia shouted as he leapt up and ran down the ravine toward the sound of gunfire.

***

At the command post, the battalion commander's meeting was ending when a radioman ran up to Captain McFarley, commander for Alpha Company. Sergeant Keller was by his side.

"Sir, 2nd Squad of 1st Platoon is returning from a patrol, about a click out. They're taking heavy fire—mortar and machine guns. 1st Squad took off to help 'em," the radioman excitedly blurted.

"Who authorized that?" hissed McFarley. "Goddamned Garcia. He's gonna get those boys killed. I should've listened to you, Joe, and demoted that boy a long time ago," McFarley snarled as he ran down the road toward his own makeshift company command post.

"Captain, let me take 3rd Squad out and get them," Sergeant Keller said, running alongside his commanding officer.

McFarley stopped and faced his platoon sergeant. "Joe, if the VC's got 2nd Squad pinned down with mortars and machine guns fire so close to our base, why don't they finish them off? It's a trap. They're baiting us to send another squad out there."

"Maybe, sir, but my brother's out there," the sergeant said starkly.

"All right, go, but hurry. You have fifteen minutes before I call in an artillery strike on those bastards. If the VC get any closer to the FOB with those mortars, they'll be in range of the battalion command post. I won't let that happen. You hear me? Get them and get back, but do it quickly!"

"Yes, sir, understood."

The sound of machine gun fire grew louder as 1st Squad made it to the ravine. As silently as they could, the eight men traversed the murky, brown water at the bottom of the defile and began to make their way up the bank on the other side of the ravine.

Harry was the first to see it: movement, forty meters to his right, on top of the embankment. He turned to the others and pointed.

"I bet that's them," he said in a loud whisper, hoping the movement was 2nd Squad trying to make it down the hill and back to camp. The men of 1st Squad fanned out as they crept toward their comrades. Then Harry saw his friend Bob Harvitz from 2nd Squad hiding behind a tree, returning fire while trying to bandage another wounded soldier's bleeding head with his other hand.

"Bobby! It's me, Harry. I got 1st Squad here to help. Hold on, buddy," Harry called out.

From behind him, he heard Garcia yell, "Come on, boys, let's go get some VC!" To Harry's shock, Garcia ran headlong past him, heading for the exposed hilltop. Two other members of 1st Squad followed.

"No!" Harry yelled, seconds too late. Machine gun fire from three sides took down Garcia and the others with him. Harry choked back nausea at the sight of the men being cut to shreds. Averting his eyes, he belly crawled toward the remaining survivors of 2nd Squad, what was left of his own squad trailing behind him. After what seemed like an eternity, Harry made it to the tree where Harvitz was kneeling.

"Bobby, who's left?"

"It's just me and Sam here. Tony's over there by those rocks. I couldn't get to him, but I know he's hit bad," answered Bobby frantically, firing blindly into the jungle all around him. "Damned VC's got us pinned down! They're everywhere!"

"They're not down in the ravine between us and the base. We can backtrack the way we came in," Harry said. "Let's get ready to move. Dan, help Bobby with Sam. Rick, you and I need to get over to those rocks to get Tony. The rest of you, give us some serious suppressive fire. Got it? Let's move," he commanded as he took off through the trees with Rick.

They didn't make it very far before a mortar round hit the rocks where Tony was sheltering. As Harry hit the ground, he saw Tony's leg fly past him. A hail of machine gun fire sprayed leaves and dirt around him, some bullets just inches from Harry's head. Terrified and thinking only of surviving, Harry scrambled as fast as he could behind a fallen log. Just as he reached the log, two bullets tore into his right thigh and knee. Harry screamed as he felt the burn of the rounds ripping into his flesh.

Behind the log, Harry looked around for help, but he was alone. He could see Rick's bloodied body ten feet behind him. Harry quickly placed a tourniquet above his knee to slow his own bleeding.

Time came to a standstill as Harry crouched behind the log. The gunfire had stopped. *They probably think I'm dead*, Harry thought. *Well, I might as well be.* He waited, weapon ready. Then Harry thought he heard voices behind him coming from the ravine. He looked down the hill, hoping to see his saviors emerge. His heart leapt as he saw movement in the trees. *Reinforcements from the FOB. Has to be.*

Harry saw a score of Vietnamese soldiers emerge from cover on top of the hill and run down toward the Americans emerging from the ravine.

"Bastards!" he cried. *They were waiting there the whole time. It's a trap. Garcia, that idiot!*

Then he heard the unmistakable sound of an M60 machine gun. Harry ducked a fierce barrage of fire and watched, astonished, as the American bullets shredded the Vietnamese troops running down the hill.

Sergeant Keller charged out of the trees to the left of the ravine with a squad of men behind him, furiously firing at anything that moved. He had set his own trap for the VC, sending a few of his men through the ravine to draw out the VC while he waited with his remaining force to ambush the attacking enemy.

The reinforcements made their way to Harry's position. Sergeant Keller jumped down behind the log with his brother. "Joe, am I glad to see you," Harry exclaimed. He saw the relief in his brother's face, but he also saw something he had never seen before—*fear*.

"What's the situation, Harry?" he asked.

"We got VC on the hilltop, small arms and machine guns. Mortar rounds coming in from the north. Not far off—I can hear them being loaded. What's left of 1st and 2nd squads are down there, behind those trees." Harry pointed into the ravine.

"Okay. Artillery strike is coming in ten minutes; let's get out of here. Corporal Wang, get the platoon together and get the wounded down to the ravine," the sergeant ordered. "Don't wait for me."

"What? Where are you going?" Harry asked incredulously. He knew they were hopelessly outnumbered and outgunned. Their only chance was to slip back down the ravine and return to base with what was left of the platoon.

"No time to explain, Harry. Wang, you have your orders!"

Sergeant Keller jumped up and ran into the unknown in front of him.

"Joe, no!" Harry screamed after his brother as Wang's hands grabbed him and started hauling him away. "Don't!"

CHAPTER NINE

LAUREN SAT SPEECHLESS LISTENING to her uncle recount her father's heroics. For the first time in her life, she saw him cry. Uncle Harry was always cool in the courtroom. He exuded confidence and was unflappable, never shaken by any curveball another lawyer threw at him. Today, however, she saw an old man twisted by painful memories.

"It was the longest ten minutes of my life. I'm not even sure how we made it back down that ravine. It was all noise, gunfire, screaming. At one point, there were just a few Cong between us and the ravine. 3rd squad was fighting them hand to hand with knives and bayonets. I heard grenades going off up in the woods. Finally, we reached the ravine. Everything was deathly quiet. I sat there in the cold water, trembling like a schoolgirl.

"I had no idea what had happened to Joe. I watched the woods intently, searching for any signs of life. Finally, some bushes stirred. My hands were shaking as I raised my rifle to fire, thinking it was VC. But it was your father—covered in blood.

"Joe walked up to me and picked me up. Without saying a word, he carried me back to camp just as the artillery strike began. He never told me exactly what happened up there, but he somehow managed to get to the mortar positions and silence them. Like the captain said, they were getting ready to shell the FOB. Joe saved a lot of people that day.

"The 3rd squad, with Joe in the lead, killed all the VC in those woods. But it was costly. We lost more than half our platoon. Captain McFarley put your father in for a Silver Star for his actions. The whole platoon thought he should have gotten something more."

Harry sighed. "That was the end of my tour in Vietnam and career in the Army," he said, pointing to his leg. "Compared to a lot of guys, I got off easy. But I know Joe never forgave himself for not being there to stop Garcia. And for me getting hurt. After that, every once in a while when he'd come home on leave, I would catch him looking at my leg. I used to limp pretty badly. I spent months in rehab to get rid of my limp just so Joe would stop feeling so guilty." He stopped talking and looked up at the clock. "It's late. Don't you want to go home and get some sleep?"

"Not yet," Lauren said. "Is that when you came home and went to college? Why didn't Dad do the same thing?"

"Yep, I went to Penn State on the GI Bill. But your father chose to make the Army a career. As for why, I think he was trying to make amends for not being there the day I got hit. Maybe he felt the longer he stayed in the fight, the more lives he could save. Or maybe he wanted to get shot himself for penance. I don't know. When Mom and I saw him a year later, he was a changed man. Stronger, more confident, yet darker and distant. He was never the same after Vietnam."

Harry stood, needing to change the subject. "You may not be tired, but I am. I'm an old man. It's been a long day and I'm going home. How long are you going to be in town?" he asked.

"A day or so, maybe. I have to get back to the hospital as soon as I can," Lauren said, hoping her uncle would not ask her why. *So many fires I have to put out.*

"So soon? Your mom needs you, Lauren."

"I know, but I have a lot of people depending on me, Uncle Harry. Not just here. I'll stay as long as I can. But what I'd like to do is get Dad transferred out of this place."

Harry winced. "You don't think Doug's taking good care of him?"

"I'm sure Doug Spiva is a good doctor, but he's a small-town country doctor, not an intensivist at a regional medical center. Dad needs critical care medicine and I don't think Hope Memorial has the facilities to pull him through this."

"You think he can get better?" Harry said. "Doug said—"

"That's just it. Dr. Spiva has given up. I am not ready to do that," Lauren said. "I'm sending Dad's films to a specialist first thing in the morning. If there's any hope, he'll know what to do."

Harry looked thoughtful, then smiled. "Maybe you're right. I'm just a lawyer. What do I know? I only sue you guys," he said playfully.

"That you do . . . snake," Lauren chuckled.

"Well, this old snake is going home. Give your mamma a hug for me. Tell her I'll call her in the morning."

"Will do, Uncle Harry. See you tomorrow."

Lauren watched her uncle's slight limp as he left the room. *Odd that I never noticed that before.*

She thought about Uncle Harry's story about her father in Vietnam. She knew her dad had served in the war, but the man lying in front of her in the hospital bed had experienced horrors that she could never imagine.

***

By her preteen years, Lauren had become convinced her father loved the military more than his own family, or why else would he have left them so often, for so long? She had tried so hard to win his approval to make him love her enough to stay around. Now, she had perspective. *Is* that *why I've always been so driven?* She looked at the still face, and suddenly she was angry. *Well, it didn't work, did it? You still left.*

She remembered her resentment at being forced to move to Hope. She'd been angry that her father didn't know her well enough to see how much she loved living in the DC area, that he didn't care about *her* wishes. But she still wanted his approval, and she'd worked hard to succeed at everything she did to earn it. *That didn't work either.* All he seemed to want was for her to change like he had and to get her hands dirty in the garden with him.

Lauren looked at her hands. She was scrupulous, as any doctor needed to be, about keeping them clean, free of germs that might infect her patients. As she stared down at them, tears dropped onto her open palms.

She remembered coming across a box of medals once while looking through the attic for an old textbook. She hadn't known what they were for, but there were a lot of them. At the time, she could not comprehend why people would spend their lives in the military for such little pay and even less respect. Plus, military life destroyed families.

Uncle Harry's story changed her harsh condescension, providing a glimpse of what might have motivated her father. *The medals were to honor him,* she thought. He had saved lives, just as she did in the hospital. Their methods were different, but the motivation was the same. Yet he had risked so much in the process.

But why, then, had he left that career to spend his days with his hands in the dirt, doing menial labor here in Hope after he retired? He was still a young man when they moved back here. Lauren shook her head, looking at his strong hands lying inert on the blanket.

"I don't understand, Dad," she said out loud. "Why?"

CHAPTER TEN

THE CHIRPING OF BIRDS slowly brought her out of her deep slumber. Lauren stretched on the twin mattress and yawned. She felt a calm she had not experienced in a long time as the rays from the morning sun warmed her face in the comfort of her old bed. She grinned wryly at the irony of having spent one of the most restful nights of her life in the bedroom she'd longed for years to escape. She lay a few minutes longer, listening to the tick of the analog wall clock providing a rhythmic counterpoint to the birdsong outside. Then she sat up and admired the dust particles dancing in the sunbeam coming through the window.

It was nearly eight in the morning. She hadn't slept that late in a long time. Usually she was up before dawn, at the hospital by six, and worked late into the evening. It was unusual that she even saw the sun, let alone a beautiful sunrise, she thought as she climbed out of bed and looked out her window. She couldn't place the type of birds that were dancing in the trees, gracefully hopping from one budding branch to the next, but their song was truly beautiful. As a teenager she'd been bored by the tranquility of country life; but at the moment she appreciated the serenity of this country home.

She surveyed the bedroom. Her parents had not changed a thing since her high school days, and it struck her that there was nothing girlie about it at all. There were no posters of teenage heartthrobs on the walls, no fluffy cushions or stuffed animals. Instead there was a desk with a poster of the table of elements above it. The room was plain and utilitarian. *Just like me,* she thought.

Her buzzing cellphone on the bedside table disrupted her thoughts. With a sigh, she answered.

"Chris, we've already been through this. Just stay there and take care of Joey, okay? There's really nothing you can do here," Lauren told her husband. But a voice in her head whispered, *Is there anything I can do here?* She had sat by her father's bed until midnight, racking her brain for a way to save him as she pored over his charts and analyzed every detail of the radiographic scans. The doctor in her knew the damage was extensive. There was almost no chance that Joe Keller would ever wake from his coma.

But Lauren was no quitter. This morning she would email the films to Dr. Jurgesson, hoping the noted specialist would have a cutting-edge idea about how to help her father.

"I want to come see him, Lauren. I love him too," Chris pleaded with her. "It'll be good for Joey."

"It *won't* be good for Joey," she countered. "Dad looks horrible. He's lying in an ICU bed stuck full of tubes, unconscious, with half of his brain not working."

She immediately regretted her choice of words as she heard how harsh they sounded and relented a little.

"Look, let me sort out what's happening here. I'm trying to figure out if there's any hope, if transferring him to Mass General will give him more of a chance. When I've got some answers, I'll call you, and we'll decide then. Okay?"

"Okay. We'll do it your way, as usual. Don't forget to call me later and update me on his condition," Chris curtly replied, and then hung up.

Lauren stood there holding her phone. *What does he want me to say, "Come on down and stare at my comatose father with me"?* She tried to clear her mind. Right now, she needed to focus on the task at hand. If Chris came to Hope, the issue of their failing marriage was sure to come up, and she didn't have time for that. And she really didn't want Joey's last memory of his beloved grandfather to be of him helpless and unconscious in a hospital bed. That just wasn't Joe Keller.

***

The smell of fresh-brewed coffee wafting up the stairs told her that her mother was up and making breakfast. Her mother, Audrey, had returned to the hospital for a few hours last evening to sit by Joe's bed while Lauren reviewed his case. She looked even more worn out than Lauren felt but had resisted going home until Lauren pressed: "Well, if you won't leave, I won't either." Audrey's concern for her daughter made her concede.

Lauren hoped her mother got some sleep.

After jumping into the shower, Lauren threw on a pair of jeans and a light sweater and headed down the stairs. She didn't look very professional, but, hey, this was Hope, Pennsylvania. Who was there to impress?

At the bottom of the stairs, on impulse she turned into the living room and looked around. The room was still decorated with her grandmother's furniture. Teenage Lauren had been embarrassed by how old-fashioned the room looked, but now she had to admit it had a lot of charm. The mantle above the old fireplace held several pictures. In the middle, prominently displayed, was a copy of the Christmas picture of herself with her family skiing that she had looked at just yesterday while still in Boston. She picked up the picture and examined it again. This time she noticed signs of her own aging, particularly the creases on her
forehead and around her mouth. Could it be her high-stress job that was aging her? She doubted it; she enjoyed that kind of stress and the intellectual challenges it brought.

But what about other kinds of stress? Her marriage was in trouble. So was her relationship with her son. *I've been avoiding dealing with those challenges,* Lauren admitted to herself. *I've blamed my job and the time it takes out of my day. Maybe I've been looking at it all wrong. Maybe I've been making excuses because I don't know* how *to rise to the challenges of relationships?*

Not wanting to pursue these uncomfortable thoughts, she placed the picture back on the mantle and picked up the one next to it. It was from her parents' trip to Hawaii a year ago. They were dancing, holding each other tight, flashing silly grins. Only two people so happy together and in love with each other could smile that way. She glanced over at her own family portrait again and noticed that Chris and she weren't even touching. Joey was standing between them.

She stepped back from the fireplace and looked around the room. Her parents had spent decades together, half of that time in this house. They always seemed so happy and comfortable with each other. And they'd loved her, she knew. So why had she been so unhappy here, in this house?

She thought about how angry she had been at her father as an adolescent. It wasn't just that he had retired from the military and moved them here into her grandmother's house. Or that she had been uprooted from the big city and forced to live in a backwater town. No, the real problem had been that even after her father came home for good, she felt even less connected to him. This was ironic, because he tried to spend more time with her but, at the same time, no longer pushed her to succeed.

What changed? What happened to my father?

"Was that Chris who called, Lauren?" she heard her mother ask from the other room.

Lauren put down the picture. "Yes, it was," she answered as she walked into the kitchen. The pale-yellow room was bright with sunshine. Her parents had kept the original cabinets, refreshing them with a new coat of white paint, but updated the room with new linoleum, countertops, and retro-style but modern appliances. The breakfast nook at one side held a pine table and benches made by Joe, with cushions and curtains sewn by Audrey out of a cheerful flower-patterned cloth. Daffodils and tulips filled a vase set on the table. Lauren's taste was for a more modern look, but she had to admit the kitchen was even more charming than the living room.

"When's he coming down?" Audrey asked, handing over a big mug of hot coffee, black and unsweetened as Lauren preferred it. "Sit. Have some breakfast."

Lauren obediently sat and smiled at her mother as she looked at the plate of egg-white omelet and fresh fruit. Audrey had been on a healthy-food kick for the past decade, and Lauren appreciated the results.

"He's not. It's hard for Joey to miss school and this is a busy time for Chris at work," she lied.

Audrey frowned. "I think they should come. It might help your father to have his only grandchild there. You know how close they are," she added. Lauren now regretted being too busy at work to accompany Chris and Joey on their annual summer trips to Hope to see her parents. Perhaps, had she come, she would know her father better.

When they returned to Boston, Chris would relay to Lauren how Joe always took Joey on a special trip. Sometimes they would go to a ball game, sometimes a hike in the mountains. Joey would often volunteer to work in the garden with his poppy.

Audrey pressed Lauren again about Chris and Joey coming to see Joe, "while there is still time."

"Well, we'll see," Lauren huffed. "I told Chris we'll talk about it again later today." She took a bite of omelet, which was stuffed with goat cheese and sautéed vegetables. "Mmm, this is good, Mom."

Audrey settled on the other side of the table and sipped her coffee. "How are Chris and Joey doing? It's been so long since I've seen them, and you never talk about them."

"They're fine."

"Have you been spending much time with them?"

Lauren stiffened. She had not told her parents about the separation. She had hoped it would all blow over and need never be mentioned. The divorce papers put an end to that. But her mother had an uncomfortable ability to intuit when things weren't going well. She said, not looking at her mother, "Sure, as best I can," and took another bite.

To her relief, Audrey backed off. "I'm glad you came home, honey," she said. "It's good to have you here right now."

Lauren took a breath. Time to get her mom's permission to move Joe.

"Mom, I want to show some of Dad's results to a colleague of mine at my hospital. He's one of the smartest doctors I know and his research is in the treatment of acute strokes, just like the one Dad had. He might be able to offer some advice on ways to get him better."

"Do you really think he can help?" her mother asked. "Doug told me that the stroke was a bad one, that even if your father survives, he won't be . . . the man he was," she finished in a choked voice.

"Maybe, but his chances will be better in Boston than here."

"You mean move him?" Audrey said, surprised. "Did you talk to Doug about this?"

"He's just a country doc, Mom. He doesn't know about all the high-tech procedures and cutting-edge research we're doing at Mass General."

"I wouldn't dismiss Doug so readily," Audrey replied. "His training was every bit as rigorous as yours, wouldn't you say?"

Lauren had to acknowledge this truth. She knew Doug Spiva's training was impeccable. He had graduated from Columbia and gone on to medical school and residency at Johns Hopkins. As with her uncle, she'd wondered why a man with such a prestigious medical background had settled in this small town.

"Maybe, but that was a long time ago, and I'm not sure he's kept up with the latest research. The hospital here is hardly a tier-one research center," Lauren said. "The care here just can't compare to Mass General."

"I don't know about that," Audrey replied. "Seems to me that a man might get the best care in a facility where everyone knows him and cares about him, rather than in a huge place where he's just another nameless patient."

Lauren stared at her, surprised by the steel in her usually soft-spoken mother's voice. "Joe has known Doug his entire life and trusts him completely. So do I," Audrey went on.

"Well, he said he would allow me to take copies of Dad's films if it was alright with you. He's on board with me checking out all the options," Lauren said defensively. She met her mother's eyes, saw the compassion in them, and on impulse blurted out, "I *have* to, Mom. I have to be sure we've done everything we can."

In answer, Audrey reached over and put her hand on Lauren's. "Of course you do, honey." The two women sat quietly for a moment; then Audrey stood up and took Lauren's plate to the sink, where she rinsed it off before putting it in the dishwasher. "All right. Let's see what your specialist friend thinks. We'll talk about whether or not to transfer him after we know more."

"Fair enough, Mom. But we don't have much time," Lauren said.

"There's always enough time to make the right decision, as opposed to rushing into a wrong one," Audrey answered, putting on her coat.

"Okay," Lauren said. "At least that's not a no."

CHAPTER ELEVEN

AS THEY DROVE TO the hospital through the bright spring sunshine, Audrey pointed out all the gardens along the way that Joe had tended to or created. Lauren began to feel that she was on a scenic tour—*Gardens by Joe Keller. He certainly put his mark on the town,* she thought. And the tour wasn't finished when they reached the hospital.

"Do you see those butterfly bushes over there?" Audrey asked, pointing to a row of tall shrubs along the front of the hospital. "They aren't flowering just yet, but in deep summer they are a wonder, pink to lilac to deep purple."

Audrey exited the car and walked to the curb and stood looking at the row of bushes. "Your father planted them after you got accepted into residency in Boston. He always loved butterfly bushes," she said pensively. "He said they brightened up any garden, not just for their own flowers but because they truly do attract butterflies."

"Mom, we should go in," Lauren said. "I want to get those films to Dr. Jurgesson as soon as I can."

Audrey looked at her daughter thoughtfully and didn't move. "You know, he never said it. But I know he planted them, specifically here at the hospital, for you."

"For me? Why?" Lauren asked. "It's not like I ever came here."

"I think he hoped that you, like the butterflies, would return home."

Lauren rolled her eyes and walked toward the entrance. Trust her mother to put some magical fantasy on a bunch of bushes just because her husband had planted them.

"I'm going to get myself some more tea. Do you want anything?" Audrey asked, stopping at a small coffee stand in the hospital foyer.

"No, thanks, Mom. I'll meet you upstairs," replied Lauren. She did usually drink two cups of coffee each morning, but felt surprisingly refreshed as she walked up the two flights of stairs and purposefully into the ICU. This time an auburn-haired nurse who appeared to be about forty was sitting at the nurses' station. She looked up and asked, "Good morning. Can I help you?" as Lauren approached the desk.

"I'm Dr. Keller. I need to arrange for files of the CTs and MRIs from bed three to be sent out."

The nurse looked her up and down. "I don't know you. You're not a physician here, and if you *are* a physician, you'd know I can't do any such thing without an order by the treating physician."

"I am a physician," Lauren snapped. "I'm an attending at Massachusetts General in Boston. Dr. Spiva has granted me access to those films. So yes, you can do what I ask. And will."

The nurse stood and pulled out Joe's chart. "There's no note from Dr. Spiva about this," she said.

"What? He must have left word with someone," Lauren protested, surprised.

"Well, he hasn't. So, there's nothing I can do," the nurse replied sternly. "Dr. Spiva should be here any moment; you can discuss it with him. Now if you'll excuse me, I have to see to a patient." She turned her back on Lauren and walked into one of the ICU rooms.

Lauren stood there, baffled and angry. She'd never been treated so dismissively by a nurse. Nurses were supposed to hop to and obey doctors without question!

Audrey came up beside her. "What's wrong?" she asked, seeing the distraught look on her daughter's face.

"Doug said he'd give me Dad's films, but that nurse can't find any notes from him authorizing the release. At least, that's what she *says*," Lauren said shortly.

"You don't believe her? Maureen wouldn't lie. Nor would she miss something like that. She's competent and thorough," Audrey replied. "Doug often says she's the best nurse he's ever worked with. Maybe Doug hadn't gotten around to it yet?"

Lauren took a deep breath. She knew HIPAA laws that protected a patient's privacy were strict. But why hadn't Doug Spiva followed through on his promise?

"Good morning," came a voice from behind her. Lauren turned to see the man in question striding down the corridor toward her. "I just came from radiology. They're making the copies you asked for. I made the request last night, but of course we don't have office help here after hours. It shouldn't take too long to put everything on a couple of disks for you."

I should have realized, Lauren thought. *No 24/7 staffing in this country hospital.*

"Oh, good morning, Doctor," said the auburn-haired nurse. Ignoring Lauren, she gave Dr. Spiva a concise report on the status of all the current patients in the ICU, then added in a matter-of-fact tone, "Also, Dr. Keller here says you authorized her to take her father's films, but I didn't hear anything about that in my pass down."

"That's fine, Maureen, thank you," Dr. Spiva answered. "I just came from radiology. The disks should be up here anytime now."

"Well, if that's all you needed, Doctor, I can pull them up on the system and email them wherever you want," replied the nurse.

"Aren't you handy with the computer," he replied.

"The new system lets us download the files ourselves no problem. Dr. Keller, give me a minute to bring up the films and you can tell me which images to send."

To her surprise, Lauren found herself rethinking her opinion of the nurse.

"Thank you," she said, returning the smile. "You see, he's my father and—"

Maureen nodded. "No worries. I understand. Let's get those files sent."

After emailing the images as an attachment to Dr. Jurgesson, Lauren went into her father's room where her mother already sat next to her father, holding his hand. Lauren conducted a quick neuro check on her father, confirming what the nurse had reported earlier: Patient Keller's condition had not changed overnight. Lauren stepped back and watched as her mother stroked her husband's hair and called out his name.

"Do you think he hears me?" Audrey asked, turning to her.

"I don't know, Mom. There's some evidence that people in comas do hear what's said around them," Lauren said. Privately she doubted it, but she knew it comforted people to think their loved ones, no matter how deeply comatose, knew they were there.

"It's so hard to see him like this," Audrey murmured, sitting on the side of the bed. "He's always been so—so vital." She looked at Lauren. "You've heard the story of how we met, haven't you?"

"Something about meeting at Fort Bragg? I don't really recall," Lauren said, sitting. It might soothe Audrey to tell the story, and it would pass the time as she waited for Jurgesson's call.

"Yes, Fort Bragg in North Carolina. It was 1972," Audrey began. "He was stationed there. I was in my last year of college in Raleigh, working on my BA in psychology. My senior thesis was about depression and high rates of suicide among the soldiers coming back from Vietnam. Now we call it post-traumatic stress disorder, of course, but in 1972 we just called it stress-reaction. It's ironic that we come up with a new name for the same condition after every war—shell shock, battle fatigue, combat stress—but still fall so short on treating it. Like most people my age back then, I was against the war, but I felt a call to help the soldiers coming back."

Lauren nodded.

Audrey continued. "The psychiatrists usually focused on the more elaborate psychiatric cases, such as schizophrenia, bipolar disorder, and psychosis. The soldiers coming back were anxious, depressed, and angry—but not psychotic. They got treated for their physical wounds, but not the scars in their minds or on their souls. It seemed to me that if I became a counselor, I could help fill this gap.

"I used to go to the military hospital at Fort Bragg and interview the soldiers returning from Vietnam. I remember the day I first saw your father like it was yesterday. I was on the postsurgical ward talking to a new arrival. I looked up and saw this tall, good-looking guy in uniform talking to some of the patients at the other end of the ward, making them laugh. He even got the ones who *never* talked to respond to him. I didn't know who he was or what he was doing there, but"—Audrey smiled at the memory—"I was instantly intrigued."

CHAPTER TWELVE

1972, Fort Bragg, North Carolina

"I'M SORRY YOU HAD to go through such hell," Audrey said softly to the young soldier, touched by his story. Her mawmaw would be rolling in her grave back in Carolina to hear her Audrey using such language. But, in truth, there was no other word for what the young corporal whom she was interviewing had been through.

She was visiting the open ward of the postsurgical unit at the military hospital on Fort Bragg, one of the largest Army bases in the country. Many of troops serving in Vietnam were sent over from this base. As she sat by the bed of the young wounded corporal, she looked around the room. There were close to two dozen other beds, each with a wounded soldier. Many were lying motionless, staring off into space. It had been a bad month in Vietnam.

Corporal Dwayne Washington was from the South Side of Chicago. He was only nineteen and had been in Vietnam for almost a full year before he lost his leg to a land mine, less than one month before he was slated to leave Vietnam. If he had not been on patrol that day, so close to his rotation back home, he would be upright. Death and mayhem did not care what a soldier's orders said.

Soldiers returning from Nam with amputations were difficult to treat. The challenges of living the rest of one's life as a cripple were bad enough, but such men were a constant reminder to citizens of an unpopular, unconventional war. Audrey wished she could ban television and newspapers from the ward; the media was full of protests against the war, and she could see how such news wounded the already traumatized veterans. Corporal Washington had been reading such an account when she arrived, and had shown it to her and asked, "What do you think about this?"

Audrey cringed as she read the anti-military article. "It may not seem like it, but there really are many of us who care about you all. I believe most of these people who may not like what our government is doing in Vietnam still support and appreciate what you have done and the sacrifices you've made."

Audrey spoke solemnly but was pleased that Washington was finally opening up and talking to her. Audrey made a point to visit him every day, and after a few days he began replying to her.

"Thank you for saying so, ma'am, but it's just so hard to believe. I mean, I read the papers here in the hospital and they roll me down to the day room each afternoon and I watch TV. All over people are protesting me and all the other guys over there. It's bad enough Charlie wants to kill you, but to come home and have your own people hate you as well is just too much to bear sometimes," said the wounded soldier, fighting back the tears.

Audrey nodded, unsure of what to say. She looked around the ward and saw the tall stranger talking to another soldier who had not spoken a word. Now, to Audrey's amazement, the wounded warrior was sitting up speaking to the tall handsome sergeant. They were even laughing!

"Look at that man, Dwayne," she said, pointing out the visitor. "He cares. Why else would he come here and talk to the men?"

"You mean Staff Sergeant Keller?" Corporal Washington said, straining to see the man she was referring to. "Yeah, he's a great guy."

"You know him?" Audrey asked.

"Sure, he came by and spent about an hour with me yesterday. He even snuck me in some candy. Don't tell the doctors or they'll punish me with an enema," Washington joked. It was the first time Audrey had seen the young corporal smile.

"I won't tell, I promise. Were you and Staff Sergeant Keller together in Vietnam?"

"No. I never saw him before yesterday. He just walked up to me, introduced himself to me and thanked me for my service. He didn't say too much about himself, just hung out with me for a while. We played cards. He let me cheat. Real nice guy," the corporal said, watching the tall visitor humor another injured soldier.

Audrey also stared at the stranger. Suddenly he looked up, met her eyes, and after a pause, gave her a warm smile. Audrey felt her heart flutter. She looked down and caught sight of her watch. It was getting late, and she had a two-hour drive to get back up to Raleigh.

"I've got to go, Dwayne," she said. "But I'll see you tomorrow, okay?"

"That would be real nice of you," the young man answered.

Audrey stood and looked around, but the sergeant had gone. *Maybe I'll see him tomorrow,* she thought, as she headed toward the hospital lobby.

"Hello," came a soft voice from behind her.

Audrey gasped. She turned. "Lordy! Do you always sneak up behind people and scare them?" she asked, smiling to let him know she was joking.

"No, I usually hide in closets and jump out at them, but I couldn't find a closet this time."

They both laughed. Audrey felt immediately comfortable with this man.

"I saw you on the ward earlier. Do you come here often?"

"Well, not as much as I'd like or they deserve. Many of them have no one to visit them. Some of their families are far away. Others just don't have anyone," Sergeant Keller said, looking back at the ward. "A hospital can be a very lonely place."

"I know, it's sad. I've been talking to some of the men for a few weeks now and I've heard many of their stories. Mostly about the war, but some about their sweethearts back home or the life they expect to have now. It's ironic; most of them are more afraid of going back to civilian life than they were in Vietnam," she went on. "So many tell me they used to count the days in Vietnam before they could come home. Now that they're home, many would rather be back in Vietnam with their units." *Oh gosh, I'm babbling.*

"For a lot of them, the guys they served with *are* their only family," the sergeant said. "It's hard for people who weren't there to understand, but, for the most part, you knew where you stood in Vietnam. You know who were the good guys and who were the bad guys. Here, the lines are considerably more blurred." He looked at her curiously. "You didn't serve, I'm guessing?"

Audrey smiled. "I was a Marine for a few years," she said.

"You're kidding!"

"Yes, I'm kidding," Audrey smiled. "We're a patriotic family, but my daddy would not have liked his little girl joining the military."

"Is that so? Did you want to?"

"Not really. I'm no fighter. But I do want to help others to a better life. I'm in college. I'm studying the psychological effect the war has had on these men. I'm Audrey McDaniels, by the way," she said, holding out her hand.

The tall man lightly gripped her hand. "My name is Joe Keller. Nice to meet you," he said with a smile. "From what I hear, you're doing more than studying them. The men I've spoken with have told me how nice you have been to them. You don't judge. You listen, and you care," he said.

His blue eyes were warm and inviting. Audrey realized she was staring into them, and looked away, reluctantly pulling her hand out of his clasp.

"Are you leaving now?"

"Yes, I need to get back to Raleigh," she answered. "It's a long drive."

"It might be easier on a full stomach. How about some German food? There's this guy I served with who was stationed in Germany years ago, married a German girl. They have a great restaurant just outside the main gate. What do you say?"

"I appreciate it, but I have so much work to do," she said instinctively, then cursed herself for not accepting the offer.

Joe Keller looked disappointed. "Sure. I understand. Let me walk you out to your car, at least."

"You don't need to, really," she began.

"Nonsense. It's the least I can do. Unfortunately, I don't have all the charm of your Southern gentlemen, but my mama did teach me some manners," he replied, giving her his winning smile.

"How did you know I was from the South? Is my accent that noticeable?"

"A little. But more so by the way you carry yourself. You've been to charm school," he said as he led her to the hospital exit. "I will also be so bold as to guess manners and etiquette were an important part of your upbringing. Your speech and enunciation are impeccable, and your walk and posture are better than most of my Marine friends."

"You are observant," Audrey quipped in her best Southern drawl.

"I do my best, Miss Scarlett," he answered with a bow.

Audrey chuckled. "Scarlett had dark hair."

"Yes, but she had green eyes like you," Joe replied. "Eyes a man couldn't look away from. And plenty of spirit to go with her beauty."

Audrey dimpled at the compliment as her heart soared. *Dinner would be nice*, she thought as they reached her car. "You say the German food is good?"

"The best this side of the Rhine," Joe answered.

"How about I follow you in my car?"

"Sounds great. If we get separated, it's on the right just outside the main gate. Look for the sign that says *Gretchen's*."

"Okay," she replied with a smile. *I really should get back to Raleigh . . . but he's so nice. And so good-looking!*

***

Joe was leaning against his car as Audrey pulled her old Plymouth up next to him in the restaurant parking lot. As she put the car into park, she looked over at him and their eyes met, and both smiled. She felt as if she knew him already.

Joe opened her door. "Dinner awaits, my lady," he said with a smile and a bow. Audrey stepped out of the car and admired the rustic Bavarian architecture of the building. She had never been out of the States, but the structure in front of her was just how she pictured a chalet in the Alps would look like.

"Is there really a Gretchen?"

"You will soon see," Joe replied and held out his arm for her to take.

Inside, Audrey was immediately transported to the fairytales of her childhood. A vast array of wooden cuckoo clocks and beer steins were artistically placed throughout the main dining room. The walls were dark paneled wood with oak arches holding up the ceiling. In the center of the large hall, rows of wooden picnic tables lined up end to end. Along the stained-glass windows were smaller tables with flickering candles and a single flower in a vase on each. The rhythmic accordion of a German oompah band played from a discreetly hidden radio. In the far corner was a bar with glasses of different colors and shapes hanging from racks overhead. The wood floors lent a perfect touch to the woodsy atmosphere. Audrey suddenly felt like Little Red Riding Hood lost in a Bavarian wood. *Is he the Big Bad Wolf?*

"You like?" Joe said softly in her ear.

She felt him behind her, his breath on her neck as he spoke. Her heart began pounding. "It's wonderful," she said.

"*Wunderbar*," he replied, taking her hand and leading her to a small table in the corner.

Joe held her chair for her as she sat down, then took his seat facing the entrance of the restaurant. Audrey couldn't help but notice that his eyes quickly surveyed the entire room before he placed the napkin on his lap and focused his attention on her. *Hypervigilant,* she had learned from her research into veterans returning from war. Sergeant Joe Keller must have been in Vietnam as well.

But even as she thought it, he seemed to relax. "Well, what do you think?" he asked.

"It's perfect, Joe. Thanks for talking me into coming."

"Well, I didn't want you to drive all the way back to Raleigh on an empty stomach."

"Very thoughtful. So, do you take all the girls here?"

"Not all. There's a strip club down the road. That's where most of them like to go. That's probably because most work there. But they don't open 'til eight and I'm hungry now."

She smiled at him. *Handsome, quick-witted, and a sense of humor.*

"Have you ever had authentic German food before?" he asked.

"No, not really."

"Well, you are in for a treat," he said, looking over her shoulder and grinning. Audrey jumped a bit as a huge man appeared at their table, threw a thick arm around Joe's neck, and held him in a mock headlock.

"Hey, buddy, they let you out of the cage today?" the man said in a raspy voice. He looked thoroughly Italian to Audrey, with thick black hair and melting dark eyes.

"Yeah, they wanted me to bring you back to the zoo with me. Your bananas are starting to pile up," answered Joe.

"Who's the lovely lady?" the man asked, glancing at Audrey.

"Tommy Dominetti, this is Audrey McDaniels. Audrey, this is Tommy. We met in the Army, right before he retired and started slinging hash for a living."

"Well, it is certainly nice to meet you," Tommy said, elbowing Joe in the arm. "Where've you been hiding this one, Joe? I gotta say, I didn't know you had such good taste."

"Stop it, you big lug. You should be ashamed of yourselves, talking that way in the presence of a lady," said a statuesque blonde of about forty years as she came up to the table. She had a noticeable German accent.

"Sorry, ma'am," Tommy answered, winking at Audrey.

"Not at all," replied Audrey politely. "I have brothers. I'm used to it. Hi, I'm Audrey. You must be Gretchen. Joe told me what a wonderful cook you are."

"Very kind," she answered, smiling. "A friend of Joseph's is always welcome here." Turning to Joe, she added, "And how are you?" Her knowing expression was one of concern, and Audrey wondered why.

"Couldn't be better," Joe replied, glancing at Audrey.

Gretchen smiled again. "I have schnitzel cooking in the back. I'll have some sent out to you two along with some spaetzle I've been working on. You'll love it." She nudged Tommy. "Come on, Thomas, let's give them some privacy,"

"What? But I haven't seen Joe in months. Joe, I've been wanting to ask—"

"Thomas," Gretchen said, her eyebrows raised and her accent a bit more Germanic. She glanced meaningfully at Audrey.

Tommy followed her glance and his face cleared. "Oh, I get it. Sure. Well, it was nice meeting you, ma'am. Hopefully Joe will bring you around more often."

"Don't worry, you big ape, we'll be back," Joe called after him as the couple walked away.

Audrey had to laugh. "She calls you Joseph?"

"Yeah. She's kind of formal with certain things. I'm Joseph, he's Thomas. Tommy and I served together for a year, right before he retired and opened this restaurant with Gretchen. They're good people. I remember when they got married. No one thought it would last. You see, Tommy used to be really wild, very rebellious. He was always getting into trouble, bucking the system. He went through women like crazy. Until he met Gretchen, that is. She tamed him without even trying. He loved her so much, he stopped his womanizing and all of his wild ways. Don't get me wrong, he's still been known to toss back a few beers a couple of times a week. But now, instead of throwing barstools when he's drunk, he teases Gretchen like the lovesick puppy he is.

"When Tommy first told me he was retiring to open a restaurant, I was skeptical. He didn't know anything about running a restaurant. But he told me that he can do anything with Gretchen in his life. I've seen Tommy literally break men with his bare hands. But you saw how he jumps when she speaks. It's hilarious. I've never seen him smile more, laugh harder, and be happier than now, with Gretchen in his life."

They both looked over at the older couple standing by the bar. Gretchen playfully hit Tommy in his big, barreled chest, obviously feigning protest at something he said to her. They could hear Tommy's laugh across the room.

"He once told me he'd be nowhere without her love. I don't know if I believe that, but I know she is his life."

Audrey noticed the expression on Joe's face as he watched his friends. At that moment she knew she was going to marry the man across from her at the table. When Joe looked back at her, she had the strangest feeling that he knew it too.

"How long have you been in the Army?" Audrey inquired, trying to change the subject.

"About five years now," Joe replied.

"How long were you in Vietnam?" she asked, then instantly regretted it. His warm demeanor suddenly changed, becoming distant, as if his thoughts were miles away from the restaurant. She had seen that look on dozens of soldiers in the hospital.

"I'm sorry, Joe. I didn't mean to be intrusive."

"It's okay," he replied, his smile returning. "I've met some great people during my time in the Army. Most of them while serving together overseas. Tommy being one of them. Good people, all with their own stories, all trying to get through life and be happy."

He seemed to notice her concerned expression, and his smile

grew more natural.

"I'm not denying Nam was tough. But I had an edge over most of the grunts there." He pulled out a small medallion he wore around his neck. "My mother gave me this when I was a teenager. It's St. Jude."

"I always get my saints mixed up. Is St. Jude for luck?" she asked, examining the old, tarnished silver medallion hanging from a metal chain.

"St. Jude is the patron saint for desperate situations. My mom used to tell me when things got tough, pray to St. Jude and he would show you the way through any dark times you might have. I don't know how true it is, but I know I made it through some rough times in Vietnam that I probably shouldn't have." Once again the faraway look came over his face. "So, you're studying psychology?"

"Yes. I want to go into counseling and work with post-trauma patients."

"Really? Why's that?"

Audrey wasn't entirely sure. "I just think there's a lot of suffering out there. I want to do what little I can to make people feel better and live happier and fuller lives. Everyone deserves that."

"Well, you're making me happier right now," he replied, looking deeply into her eyes. She didn't expect the comment and felt the warm tingling in her face as it turned pink.

"Sergeant Keller, I do declare," she said, fanning herself with her napkin. "I believe you are making me blush."

Joe smiled. "I think St. Jude has come through for me again," he said quietly.

Chapter Thirteen

LAUREN SAT MESMERIZED AS her mother continued on about that chance meeting that blossomed into a lifetime commitment.

"We dated for about a year before we were married. You were born just over one year after that. I remember trying to come up with a name for you. Then your father suggested 'Lauren,' after one of his best friends. I believe you saw him yesterday?" Audrey said.

"Do you mean that scary-looking man that was here when I arrived?"

Audrey laughed. "That scary-looking man is one of your father's most loyal friends. He's a real good man. His name's Mike Laurence. You didn't remember him?"

"He said we'd met before," Lauren replied. "But no, I don't remember him."

"It's been a long time since you've seen him, Lauren. But Mike was—and still is—your father's best friend."

"How could I not know Dad's closest friend?" Lauren asked, more to herself than to her mother.

"Your visits home never coincided with his visits, I guess," Audrey answered. Lauren wasn't sure if that was a reproof for how infrequently she had visited her folks. But Audrey went on.

"Mike's still in the military. He travels a lot, but he stays in touch. We see him at least once or twice a year. After Robbie Pearson—do you remember Robbie? Used to live across the street? He's now the sheriff of Hope. Anyway, after Robbie showed up on my doorstep to tell me about your father being found unconscious, I called you, and then I called Mike. Mike was in North Carolina, but he took leave and drove straight here without even stopping to pack first."

Lauren was silent. She had not known that her father had a friend like that, a friend who would drop everything just to be with him in a time of need. It seemed Joe Keller inspired deep loyalty, not just in his brother, but in others who knew him as well. There were depths to her father she had never seen. *Why?*

"Mom," she found herself asking, "was I a good daughter?"

"Why, Lauren," Audrey replied softly, putting her hand on her daughter's knee. "You're a strong woman, a caring mother, *and* a wonderful daughter. You work so hard at making people's lives better and relieving their suffering. We're both very proud of you."

"But do I do it for the right reasons?" Lauren asked rhetorically. "Am I only doing it for the prestige?" She looked at her mother. *After all, she's a counselor*, she thought. *She might have some insight for me.* "Ever since you told me about Dad, I've been thinking about why I've been working so hard. I don't know if I have an answer. Maybe I was just always trying to get Dad's approval."

"Only you can answer that, dear," Audrey said after a moment of reflection. "I know Joe wasn't always the best at letting you know how he felt about you. But as for having his approval, I can tell you that your father bragged about you to everyone he met. He would pull out your picture to show them. But he never said, 'This is my daughter, the doctor' when he showed your picture. Do you know how he described you to strangers?"

"No, how?" Lauren asked, feeling oddly anxious.

"He would say, 'This is my Rennie. She's smart as a whip, a hard worker, has a beautiful family, and is a good daughter. I wish I could be half the person she is.'"

Lauren stared at her mother in disbelief. "My father wanted to be like me? I always thought . . . I thought he wanted me to be more like *him*."

"Oh no, honey." Audrey paused for a minute, as if gathering her thoughts. "Your father knew that we all have our own obstacles to face and lessons to learn. He had to face his and you're no different. Life is hard, Lauren, and we have to learn from our mistakes in order to grow. Some people can't do that, but you can—and have. You're fearless about facing up to things, just like your father. He knew that. Your father could always see the person you would become. That was his special gift. He could look deep into people and see their goodness and strengths. And because of that, he could bring out the best in people."

"But he wasn't always there for me, back then," Lauren said. "All those years before we moved back to Pennsylvania, I barely remember him. He wasn't there when I was growing up. All my classmates had both parents around at school functions, but I didn't. I couldn't even tell them what my father did, except that he was in the Army. And then when he came home, I don't remember him acting like I was special, like all my success in school meant anything." Lauren heard her voice rising, took a breath, and tried to calm down. "You tell me he was proud of me, but he didn't tell *me* that. He just tried to get me to work in the garden with him after we moved here, like that was more important."

Was he outside hoping I'd join him there, all the time I was inside, wishing for him to come to me?

"I'm not making excuses for him, Lauren. Your dad had his own demons back then, but he spent as much time with you as he could. He thought, as I did and still do, that you sometimes pushed yourself too hard. He told me once that he was afraid to praise you too often because he thought that would encourage you to push even harder. What he wanted to teach you was how to relax, how to live life for the moment. That was a lesson that took him nearly forty years himself to learn, and he wanted you to learn it sooner than he had.

That's one reason why we moved here, so your father could relax and enjoy life." She smiled ruefully. "I did try to tell him that you had to walk your own path, not his, but Joe's biggest flaw was always thinking he knew what was best for others."

***

Lauren had always believed that her mother worshipped her father, just as he worshipped Audrey. It had annoyed her to see how high a pedestal each placed the other on. Their marriage had seemed like a textbook case of codependency, which Lauren thought lay behind most cases of so-called "true love."

Lauren stood and kissed her mother on the cheek. She needed time to digest all that she had learned, and she had work to do.

"Thanks, Mom. I'm going to try to reach Dr. Jurgesson now. He should have had time to look at Dad's scans. Then I'll come back and we'll talk about a plan."

Audrey looked up at Lauren, then down at her husband. She gave a little shake of her head, but said only, "Okay, I'll see you later."

CHAPTER FOURTEEN

LAUREN WALKED OUTSIDE THE hospital to make her phone call. The bright morning had kept its promise and the temperature outside was pleasantly warm. But before Lauren could dial Jurgesson's number, the phone rang. "Dr. Keller," she answered.

"Hello, Lauren. It's Anna Novotny. How's your father doing?" her new boss asked politely.

"Hi, Anna. Thanks for calling. He's the same, I'm afraid. He had a massive CVA and is unresponsive."

"I'm so sorry to hear that. And I'm sorry to be interrupting, but I do have to ask something. How long do you think you'll be there?"

Anna was not just asking out of personal concern, Lauren knew. She needed to make sure she had enough staff to cover the work.

"I'm not sure. I sent his films to Jurgesson this morning; I was just going to call him to see what he thinks about transferring him to Mass Gen."

"I'm afraid I have bad news for you, then. Hans is away for the day presenting at a conference. Do you want me to have someone else look at the films?"

Damn. Lauren thought for a moment. She had to be evasive, not wanting to slight her boss. "Dad wasn't found for hours, so we're well past the urgent window. Will Hans be back tomorrow?"

"Yes, he will. Well, I hope you know all of us here are very concerned about you and your family," Anna said.

"Thank you, I appreciate that."

There was a brief pause. "I don't want to pressure you, Lauren, but you know we have the research seminar coming up and we're not quite ready for it. You remember tabling some agenda items for the next meeting, which is scheduled tomorrow afternoon? We need to get to them. We still have much work to do."

You mean I have much work to do. "I understand. I'll be back for the meeting."

"That's not what I meant. You stay as long as you need to. I just wanted you to know that, given that you might be away longer than a day or two, I'm going to have Dr. Hernandez handle the research committee for now. He's been a big help to me during my transition and I think he'll do a fine job covering for you."

Lauren went cold. Luis Hernandez was a young hotshot internist from Berkeley. He had been on staff for a couple of years and was making quite a name for himself. For the past three months he had been lobbying hard to be put on the research committee. Lauren had no doubt that he saw her absence as an opportunity to replace her. From what she knew of the ambitious man, he'd cajole Anna into making him the new chair of the Internal Medicine department as well.

"I don't think that will be necessary," Lauren said stiffly into the phone. "As I said, I intend to come back tomorrow. I can see Hans in the morning and prepare for the meeting at one."

There was a pause. "Well, if you're sure. But if things don't go according to plan, call me." Lauren heard Anna take a deep breath. "I also need to talk to you about Dr. Sutton."

"What? Sutton?" fumbled Lauren. It took her a moment to remember that Faye Sutton had filed a complaint against her. *Was that only yesterday?* "Oh, yes? What about her?"

"I'm afraid I haven't been able to get her to drop the complaint. There's going to be an investigation."

"Are you kidding me? Is this the thanks I get for trying to teach people like her, to make them the best physicians possible? Not to mention trying to keep the hospital from getting sued when incompetent residents do stupid things that can kill patients? So what if she got her little feelings hurt."

"I understand how you feel," Anna said stoically. "But I have no choice. I'm sorry, Lauren, but I have to follow protocol." She took a breath and said in a softer tone. "It's rotten timing, I know."

"You have no idea," muttered Lauren. *Dad and my marriage are falling apart all at once—and so is my job.*

"I suppose not," Anna responded. "Well, call me when you have any new information," she said. "Goodbye. And Lauren?"

"Yes?"

"All the best with your dad."

Rattled, Lauren walked around the hospital grounds for a few minutes, thinking about all the things on her plate. How was she going to solve all these problems piling up? She took a breath. *Do the most important thing first.* The most important thing was her father, so she retraced her steps and returned to the ICU.

Her mother was not in the room. Instead, the scary-looking man she'd seen the night before was sitting by her father's bed. Before she could recall his name, he stood up and introduced himself.

"Hi Lauren. I'm Mike Laurence." His hand engulfed hers.

"You're my dad's best friend. Mom was telling me about you."

"I try to be," he answered. "I'm glad to get this chance to speak with you. Your aunt showed up a few minutes ago and took your mom out for lunch. Shall we sit down?" It was more of a command than an invitation, and Lauren obeyed.

Mike took a deep breath, but instead of speaking to Lauren, he addressed his unconscious friend. "I'm breaking security protocol, but I'm doing it for you, brother. Your memory needs to be alive in your daughter. It's the least I can do for you."

Lauren stiffened.

"You see, Lauren, your father and I worked together a long time ago," Mike began. "We met in Vietnam. It was in the first few months of 1975. I had just finished Special Forces training at Fort Bragg. I was only eighteen at the time, full of myself and ready to conquer the world."

"But Dad wasn't in Vietnam in 1975. He was there earlier."

Mike smiled. "Not many people may have known it, but trust me, he was there in 1975. With me."

"That's when the war was ending, right?" From what Lauren had read, it was a time of chaos in Vietnam. "What were you doing there?"

Mike paused. "You don't need to know any of those details," he said bluntly. "The point is, that's where we met. Afterwards, Joe took me with him back to Fort Bragg. He was one of the senior instructors at the Army's newly revamped Special Warfare School. I worked for him as a hand-to-hand combat instructor." Mike took a sip from his cup of coffee. "During one of his earlier tours in Nam, he worked for a man named Greg Buckley. Late in 1977, Colonel Buckley approached your father. He was forming a new unit called Special Forces Operational Detachment–Delta. He wanted your father in the unit. Frankly, I was surprised when your father said yes. It wasn't exactly the type of work I thought your father would want."

"What kind of work was it?"

Mike didn't answer her directly. "You see, Lauren, your father wanted to be an instructor because he thought he could save lives. We saw a lot of death in that Asian jungle. It ate away at him every day. He used to tell me the better he trained his men during peacetime, the more chance they would have at staying alive in combat. My approach was different. I focused on the offensive, more aggressive art of warfare. Joe always took the cautious approach. His goal was to minimize casualties, on either side, or even avoid conflict all together. Even though we disagreed about this at the time, we were a good team, and he convinced Colonel Buckley to take me into the new organization with him. I remember when he told me Colonel Buckley agreed to bring me on board. I was so excited, but he just looked at me sadly and said, 'There's plenty of pain and suffering out there. Don't be in such a hurry to go out to find it.' It wasn't until years later that I fully understood his words.

"We trained hard. It was nearly two and a half years before we were called upon for our first mission," Mike said, drifting off into his past.

CHAPTER FIFTEEN

November 1979, Fort Bragg, North Carolina

THE CHILL MADE STAFF Sergeant Michael Laurence shiver. He looked up to see dark clouds rolling in from the east. *A storm's brewing,* he thought. But that wasn't all. Something bad was about to happen. He could feel it. He switched his attention back to the score of young men running the obstacle course. His friend and mentor, First Sergeant Joseph Keller, stood beside him. Joe and he had very different approaches, different philosophies about what it meant to be a soldier. Joe taught his men how to reason and think, while Mike focused on physical and mental toughness. But they had the highest respect for each other.

"Alright, men, gather round," Joe bellowed in a commanding voice. Suddenly the obstacle course was empty, and Joe was surrounded by the soldiers. Mike looked at their eager faces. Most of the men had been in five to seven years, some with combat time in Vietnam. They were ready to get back in the fight. The only problem—there was no fight to go to. That was okay with Joe, Mike knew, but he understood the men's impatience. And like them, he would follow Joe Keller anywhere. But before Joe could say anything, a Jeep rolled up.

"Hey, Joe," called the crusty senior sergeant driving the Jeep. "Colonel Buckley wants to see you. You too, Laurence."

Joe nodded, calling out to one of the staff sergeants. "Why don't you take the guys on a little run?"

"Will do, Joe," the sergeant grinned. "Let's go, girlies, time for me to run you into the ground."

Mike and Joe climbed into the Jeep. Mike was surprised at the summons. Although Joe was one of the senior instructors, it was rare for him to be beckoned to the CO's office. Usually, they only met at the weekly Commander's Briefing.

The headquarters compound was tucked deep in the thick pine forests of a remote area in the northern portion of Fort Bragg. It had been hastily erected to hold these elite troops. Security was strict; even men well known to the sentries always had to produce their identification. It was made clear to anyone coming from outside that the 1st SFOD-D, Delta for short, didn't like visitors.

Colonel Buckley's office was exactly what one would have expected from the exterior of the shiny metallic Quonset hut. To one side was a collection of exotic spears and shields collected through Buckley's years of fighting wars in Southeast Asia.

Colonel Buckley was the warrior's warrior, well over six feet tall and a legend in the Army Special Forces community. He looked the part from his salt-and-pepper crewcut and the stubby cigar perpetually stuck in his mouth. His walls were adorned with awards, certificates, diplomas and pictures of far-off places. He could read others and prided himself most on building his team with the very best he could find.

Buckley first met Joe Keller in Vietnam while Joe was serving as a military advisor to the South Vietnamese Special Forces. One day, while watching Joe training the new Delta recruits, Buckley had said to Mike, "Joe's different from most special operators. He's neither aggressive nor arrogant, but rather uses his formidable intelligence to win the day. But, mark my words, there's more to Joe than meets the eye. He has compassion. Sure, he's completely dedicated to his men and his mission, but he also cares about those all around him. Believe it or not, even the enemy," Buckley chuckled. "On the firebases in Vietnam, while the other Special Forces soldiers were catching a nap in between patrols, Joe would be playing with the children or helping the villagers fix their huts."

Mike wasn't surprised that Colonel Buckley valued compassion in his warriors—the colonel was often quoted as saying, "Killing all the bad guys doesn't win wars these days. You have to win the hearts and minds of the populace."

Mike wasn't so sure about that. In his view, enemies were enemies, especially in Vietnam.

Both men came to attention as they entered the hut.

"As you were, men. Have a seat," barked Colonel Buckley. "How are your boys doing?"

Joe looked at Mike. "They're physically ready for any mission, sir," Mike reported.

"How about mentally ready?" the colonel asked.

Joe fielded this one. "Many have seen some combat, sir, but not all of them. Those that have, only took part in the closing days of Vietnam. They'll do any mission you ask them to do, sir, but they're still a little raw."

"Well, I guess you'll have to hone them up soon. This morning a group of radical Islamic students stormed the US embassy in Iran. They overtook the embassy and are holding Americans hostage. The diplomats are working on the situation, but we need to be ready in case that doesn't work."

A few days earlier, Joe had said something about how unstable Iran was becoming since the shah left the country to get his cancer treated. Joe wasn't a political man and he loved his country, but he'd told Mike how he wished their leaders would make better decisions about which dictator to back.

"The shah is a butcher," Joe said. "He's out of touch with his people; they detest him and all who support him. And that means America."

He called it right, Mike thought, and now Joe and he and their men would have to risk their lives because America bet on the wrong side. He knew what was coming next. After all, Delta was created to be America's counterterrorism force.

"What's the plan, sir?" Joe asked.

"Nothing concrete yet. I want you to work the men hard. Focus on hostage rescue for now. Desert warfare. Get them ready."

"Roger, sir. Will do," Mike and Joe replied.

As they walked back Joe said, "I don't like it. A small-scale hostage rescue mission in the heart of Tehran in the midst of a revolution? Going to be difficult to say the least. We have far too few friends left there that would be willing to help." He spat. "I've been watching the news, but the media doesn't get it. What's going on in Iran is more than just a coup. It's an entire philosophical change. They're rejecting Western ideology and returning to their core Islamic roots. Diplomacy isn't going to work in this situation. The students are too committed to their cause."

"What do you want me to do, Joe?" Mike asked.

"Take the men to the shoot house and run a few close quarter drills with 'em. I want them to be able to storm a building, clear the rooms, and safeguard hostages in under a minute while staying safe. Make sure our schedule is cleared so we can focus on this type of training for the next couple of weeks at least . . . And call our liaison with the State Department. See if he can put you in touch with a man named Sean McFarley. He works the Iranian desk. Tell him I need to get four men some Farsi language immersion training, starting yesterday. You and I plus two guys that you pick. It needs to be local in case we have to fly out at a moment's notice. Sean was my company commander during my first tour in Vietnam. He's a good guy. Tell him he owes me one and I'm calling to collect, but tell him to keep it quiet. Got all that?"

"Yeah, Joe, no problem. How soon do you think we'll be deployed?" Mike asked.

"Maybe days, maybe weeks, no way to know. But I want the men ready. After you take 'em through some tough scenarios at the shoot house, run them hard through the sandy trails." Joe walked on a few steps. "I'll see if we can let them go home to spend some time with their families before we ship out, but don't say anything about that to them. I'm not going to tell them about the mission until we have a plan. Meanwhile, I'll go through all their records again, and you and I will sit down later and talk about who we want on the team."

Joe and Mike slept very little over the next few months. They were on edge, waiting for the call to get the team to the airfield. Joe had an additional stress in that he could not tell his wife what was going on. Audrey was concerned about him, Joe told Mike, but she knew he couldn't talk about his work.

***

Finally, the day came. Joe was summoned to Colonel Buckley's office and came immediately to find Mike after that meeting. "This is it," he told his friend. Diplomatic efforts had not been able secure the release of the US hostages in Iran, and the American people were demanding that the White House do something definitive. Despite the weeks formulating a plan, Joe did not feel so confident.

"There are just too many unknowns and risks," he said. He was also frustrated because the officers had ignored most of his input while designing the operation.

Joe didn't have a problem with the basic operational aspects of the plan, which called for Colonel Buckley to go in with a couple of Delta teams to raid the US embassy in Tehran and free the hostages. They would all then get picked up by US helicopters pre-staged in the Iranian desert. What bothered Joe was the political influences on the planning. Everyone wanted a piece of the pie. As a result, US Marines would fly helos from Navy ships into the desert where they would be refueled by Air Force reconfigured cargo planes.

Joe knew that the helicopter pilots didn't have much experience flying in the desert. He had spent some time advising the Israelis during the Arab–Israeli war in 1973 and saw the difficulties they had flying combat missions in the Sinai, despite extensive training in desert operations. Sand wreaked havoc on mechanical and hydraulic systems, and American pilots rarely practiced in such an environment.

A few days before the mission launch, Colonel Buckley asked Joe and Mike to hand-pick an advance team. They chose the two other soldiers who had gone through the intensive Farsi language training—Bud Ritchie and Hector Chavez.

All of their gear had been packed and ready for months, and they left within a few hours. There was no time for Joe to run home to say goodbye to Audrey. He called her instead. When he hung up he sighed.

"It's hard explaining when you can't really explain," he said to Mike. "Audrey thinks she understands, but she doesn't, not really. How could she? But she tries. And she senses that this is going to be a bad one."

"Audrey's a special woman," Mike said.

Joe nodded. "That she is. The worst thing is I'm missing Rennie's sixth birthday. We were going to take her to the park. I've arranged for a clown and a pony to be there. Audrey will take her, but I feel rotten about missing it. I thought I'd have more time with my family in this job stateside, but it's not looking like that's going to be the case. As for the risks—" Joe shook his head. "Everything looks different when you have a kid."

**

Mike broke off his story as Lauren stood. "Are you telling me that my father regretted leaving us that long ago?" she demanded. "That he knew how hard it was on me, on us? And he *still* stayed in the Army?"

"It was his duty, Lauren. One he took seriously," Mike said gently.

"More seriously than he took his duty to his wife and child?" Lauren shot back as she turned and left the room.

Lauren bolted out of the ICU, past the nursing station and pounded down the hall. She shoved through the exit door and ran down the sidewalk. She took a deep breath of cool morning air and slowed down to a walk. *What am I doing? The nurses must be amused,* she thought. Lauren's hands shook. *Trouble at work, an impending divorce and the death of my father, a man I apparently never really knew. Anything else left to go wrong?*

Compartmentalizing pressure was a way of life for Lauren, and she had certainly been in much more stressful situations. But they were mostly professional challenges governed by the parameters of work. Personal matters were messier.

It hadn't helped to hear how her father left her and her mother, yet again, to go fight in some insignificant war. *The Iranian Hostage Crisis, for chrissakes. It wasn't even a war! And I was six. I didn't care about hostages in Tehran or soldiers in Vietnam or anywhere else. I wanted my father!*

Lauren sank onto a bench and put her head in her hands as tears rolled down her cheeks. Someplace in her heart, a place of deep hurt, had opened. She sat and let the pain flow freely.

She wasn't sure how much time passed before she was able to sit up, take a deep breath, and wipe her face. Feeling drained but calm, she looked around the place she'd never really thought of as her hometown. *But I suppose it is, if any place is.*

The buildings were old but well kept. Most of the two-story buildings surrounding the hospital were built before World War II. It was quiet, much quieter than anywhere in Downtown Boston or around her hospital. Lauren had always considered Hope's stillness a mark of a dying town, a rustbelt town with shuttered factories and lots of For Sale signs on vacant houses, a cultural wasteland.

But now she watched people going in and out of buildings, walking along the sidewalks, driving slowly past. Hope suddenly seemed vibrant.

As her gaze traveled over the hospital grounds, she noticed the butterfly bushes her mother had pointed out earlier. Something was different, though. One bush had started to bloom early, and a yellow butterfly danced gingerly around the purple spike of flowers.

Dad got his butterflies, after all.

She watched as the insect searched for its nectar, so vital for survival. The budding spike of purple wasn't open enough yet, so the butterfly flitted on to the nearby rose garden that Lauren was sure her dad must have planted as well. The insect's motion was captivating. She couldn't remember ever sitting and just watching a butterfly like this. So elegant, swooping from one flower to the next.

Suddenly, she felt a wave of peace wash over her. She stood and walked steadily back into the hospital, up the corridor to the ICU and her father's room.

"I'm ready," she said to Mike. "I want to hear the rest of the story."

I'm ready to learn more about who my father really was.

Chapter Sixteen

April 1980, Tehran, Iran

THE SMALL SPECIAL FORCES advance team entered Tehran in the middle of April 1980 using fake passports provided by the CIA. They posed as Canadian journalists covering the revolution taking place all over Iran.

Every street corner and shop was covered with graffiti and posters shouting, "Death to America." Graphic depictions of blood-soaked Americans hung next to posters of the Iranian savior, the revered Ayatollah Khomeini, while effigies of both the shah of Iran and President Jimmy Carter were burned in marketplaces and squares in downtown Tehran. Teenagers ran through the streets firing AK-47 assault rifles into the air.

Although they wore the new Iranian government-issued Canadian Press badges around their necks, the four Americans felt cold, angry stares wherever they went. Most of the CIA contacts operating in Iran during the shah's reign had been compromised after the start of the revolution and the fall of the embassy, yet there were a few still in place that were willing to help Joe and his men. The team moved into a safe house not far from the occupied embassy compound where the hostages were being held. The house was in a wealthy neighborhood and had high walls around the courtyard, good for both privacy and security. The last thing the Americans wanted to do was to draw attention to themselves before the raid.

Joe, Mike, Bud, and Hector stood around the ornate marble table in the center of the well-lit dining room. Maps were scattered over the table as the men familiarized themselves with their surroundings. In the distance, they heard gunfire as the revolutionary students celebrated their new government—or carried out executions of those that had helped the previous government.

"Mike, you and I need to get details on the number of guards and their positions on the embassy grounds. We've got to identify their exact locations, patrol patterns, and weapons. Our sources tell us there aren't any soldiers in the compound, only students. While that means their tactics will be weak, their unpredictability could prove dangerous. Bud and Hector, you two link up with our contact here in Tehran. Rent two off-road vehicles to scope out the landing fields. Mike and I will check out the embassy and we'll meet back here at 1700," he instructed his team.

"Remember, we're Canadian journalists," Joe said. "We don't want to call attention to ourselves in any way. Play it cool, Mike."

Their safe house had been deliberately chosen for being close to the US embassy grounds. Joe and Mike took a stroll through the neighborhood and slowly made their way toward the compound. There was a pedestrian square near the embassy entrance that contained a small café with outside tables.

Mike pointed to the café. "There, that might work," he told his boss.

"Okay, let's have a seat in the corner and see what we can see. Pull out your press badge and hang the camera around your neck," Joe instructed as they crossed the busy street. "Remember, we're just two reporters from Vancouver taking a coffee break," he added.

Mike complied as they reached the other side and found seats at a table outside the café that was farthest away from any other occupied table.

Joe, making use of the little French he had learned from the kids he'd played soccer with in Vietnam, ordered two cups of Iranian coffee. It was thick and bitter, and both men instantly felt the jolt from the high dose of caffeine in each cup. It felt good. They sat back, trying to blend into the wall behind them as they surreptitiously surveyed the embassy.

The two were made uneasy by the scene unfolding in front of them. Scores of teenagers in jeans and T-shirts were walking around the streets with AK-47s and hand grenades, waving their rifles in the air and chanting anti-American slogans:

"*Al-Moot Lil Amreeka! Marg bar Kartr!*"

"Down with America! Death to Carter!"

Atop the walls of the US embassy, stoic guards stood, staring at their countrymen on the streets below. They, too, wore jeans, but over their T-shirts were olive drab military vests filled with ammunition for the array of weapons they carried. Although overtly more subdued than the crowd of students chanting in the square, intense hatred burned deep in the eyes of the revolutionaries guarding the US embassy.

"This isn't going to be easy, Mike," said Joe in a low tone. "It's going to be a bloodbath."

"Hopefully it'll all be their blood," Mike replied coldly. He felt that the Iranians should pay dearly for taking his countrymen hostage and wanted to kill as many Iranians as possible before bringing his people home.

"They have families, too, Mike. We may not understand their ways, but most of them just want to get through the day, just like us," Joe murmured.

"They're *not* like us. Look at them. They're animals. They respect nothing. They're led by their emotions, not reason or logic. You of all people should recognize that."

Joe regarded the younger man for a moment.

"Are we any different?" he asked. "If a foreign government had influenced and, in essence, controlled our society for thirty years, enriching the foreigners at your expense, you might feel otherwise," he continued.

Mike could see Joe's eyes flicking as he counted the number of students on the roof.

"Come on, Joe. How can you have any sympathy for these guys at all?" Mike exclaimed.

"I don't sympathize with them. Terrorism is always wrong. Taking and holding hostages is wrong. But I won't be blinded by my patriotism, either. Mike, listen to me. Don't let your emotions cloud your mind or your judgement. You can hate what they do personally, but at the same time, you need to try to understand why they act as they do. Put yourself in their shoes. You should always try to think like your enemy. Understand their motivation. Do this, and you'll better be able to predict their moves and responses."

Mike thought about this for a moment. *Joe's right, as usual. Being ugly Americans has never got the USA anywhere. Damn, I need to focus more and put my emotions aside.* He glanced at Joe. *When will I ever stop learning from this guy?*

"Okay, I have seventeen tangos on the walls, nine on the outside perimeter. It's 4 p.m. You got their weapons down?" Joe asked.

"Roger, got it. What time are we coming back?"

Joe took a moment to reflect. "Let's try to scope things out sometime after midnight, just to see if anything's changed. The mission calls for a zero-dark-thirty insertion into the embassy compound, so we need to make sure we have an accurate picture of their nightly routine."

"Sounds like a plan. We should probably look at some of the escape routes while there's still daylight," Mike said.

"Good idea. Let's head out," Joe said, throwing some Iranian toman down on the table, paying generously for their unfinished coffee. To keep up the illusion of being Canadian, he thanked the waiter in French as the man hurried to claim the money.

They walked cautiously back to the safe house, carefully noting numerous escape routes and dangerous choke points along the way. Should the plan fail inside the city, it would be up to Joe and his three men to navigate through these dangerous streets and lead the dozens of Delta Force rescuers out of the crowded capital to safety.

That evening, the advanced team regrouped to go over what they had learned and prepare for the mission that was coming up fast. Joe pointed out landmarks on the map on the wall as he talked.

"Listen, guys, tomorrow we've got to survey the two landing zones out in the desert and get ready for the rendezvous with the boss."

Joe pointed to a spot on the map circled in red ink hundreds of miles south of Tehran. "Desert One is here. The C-130s will land at Desert One with the insertion teams to rendezvous with and refuel the RH-53D Sea Stallion helicopters coming in from the *Nimitz*. Our guys will then board the helos and fly here"—he pointed to a spot on the outskirts of Tehran—"a location known as Desert Two. Mike and I will be at Desert One. Bud and Hector, you two will wait at Desert Two with enough trucks to transport our guys into the city. We'll regroup here and go over plans for the assault before moving out. Any questions?"

"Not exactly a walk in the park. Who came up with this crazy plan?" Bud asked, eliciting a chuckle from Hector.

"I hear you, but we all have our orders," replied Joe. "Bud, were there many larger trucks available where you got the Toyotas today?"

"Sure, plenty. Don't worry, Hector and I will have enough vehicles to get all our boys back here tomorrow night," he replied confidently.

"Good. Go native in the morning and find those vehicles. After you secure the trucks, bring 'em out to Desert Two and start prepping the area for the eight helos to land. Mike, you and I will head out to Desert One in the morning to get it ready for the first rendezvous with the C-130s. Mike and I are making one more recon later tonight to check on the guards at the embassy. Bud and Hector, get some sleep. Tomorrow will be a busy day," finished Joe.

***

The next morning was hectic as the four men prepared for their long drives into the Iranian desert. Their Iranian allies, former shah supporters still on the CIA payroll, had arranged everything for them, including vehicles and press passes for travel out of Tehran.

Joe and Mike left the city first, heading south on the long drive to Desert One. Bud and Hector were lining up more vehicles in Tehran before taking the shorter trip to Desert Two just outside the capital. Once they'd reached their secret locations, there was still hours of work for all four men to turn the raw desert into temporary landing strips.

The arduous drive over harsh and barren Iranian desert took much longer than Joe or Mike had expected. Finally, they reached the coordinates for Desert One given them by Colonel Buckley. They were running out of daylight as they started to mark a long runway in the desert for the large C-130 aircraft to land on. After they had cleared the makeshift airstrip of as much debris as possible, Mike measured it and placed infrared lights and strobes at each end. These would enable the pilots to see the dimensions of the crude airstrip in the dark.

After they were done preparing the runway, it was time for the most difficult part of the mission: waiting. If all went according to the plan, their wait wouldn't be long. By Joe's calculations, the eight helicopters should already have departed the USS *Nimitz* currently floating in the Indian Ocean but, due to their slower speed, would arrive at Desert One after the C-130s.

The desert was dark and cold, but somehow beautiful, Mike thought as they waited for the planes to arrive. However, he knew all too well that at any time the stillness could be shattered by unexpected visitors.

"Stop worrying, old man. It'll be fine," Mike told him as Joe kept swiveling to look at the road and then the sky.

"The wind's picking up," answered Joe.

"They'll be here soon. Everything's going smoothly," Mike said reassuringly. But then they noticed the stars to their west begin to dim. They both watched incredulously as the night sky suddenly disappeared right before their eyes.

"Sandstorm!" Joe shouted as the howl of the wind grew louder. "Right in the flight path. How high are the birds flying?"

"Not very high. They need to come in low to avoid radar detection once they enter Iranian airspace," replied Mike.

"Damn it, they'll fly right into the storm and we can't do a damned thing about it. I can't warn them," cried Joe. Everyone on the mission was observing strict radio silence.

Then they heard the unmistakable sound of a diesel truck approaching.

"What next?" lamented Joe as he saw the headlights fast approaching from the same direction as the storm.

Mike was the first to react. "Let's go," he called out, and ran through the sand as fast as he could, heading directly for the approaching vehicle. It appeared to be a civilian bus, he noted as he jumped in the middle of the road and waved his arms in the air like a madman in the incoming lights.

The bus continued coming right for him. Mike stood his ground, raised his M16 rifle and pointed it at the driver.

"Mike, NO!" Joe yelled loud enough to be heard over the bellowing wind. "Don't shoot him!"

Mike hesitated for a moment, then lowered his rifle a couple of inches and fired a single shot. The bullet hit the right front tire and the bus rolled to a stop directly in front of Mike.

"Good job," Joe said as he caught up to his friend. He approached the bus and pounded on the door as Mike covered him with his weapon. The driver, confused and afraid, opened the side door. Joe climbed aboard, followed closely by Mike, holding his rifle in a threatening posture.

"Civilians," Joe said calmly, seeing the scared faces of several dozen passengers staring at him in horror.

"What the hell are we going to do with them?" Mike demanded.

"They stay here. First, we make sure no one has any weapons or radios. We'll keep them on the bus so they're contained. There're only two of us and I, for one, don't want to be chasing anyone in the desert tonight. Start searching the left side. I'll start with the driver then take the right," Joe ordered.

The passengers were all too afraid to speak or move. None had weapons or radios. Then Joe heard the unmistakable sound of a C-130 approaching.

"They're here," Mike said. "A little late," he added, looking down at his watch.

"The storm must've slowed 'em down. Keep an eye on the passengers while I drive the bus over to the rally point."

Mike pulled the driver out of his seat and pointed toward an empty seat near the front of the bus, which the cringing man took. Mike kept his weapon pointed toward the passengers as Joe slowly drove the crippled bus off the road towards the makeshift airstrip where the first C-130 was landing.

"Stay here and cover them while I talk to Colonel Buckley," Joe said, turning off the engine and standing up. The C-130 was turning off the strip, making room for the next plane to land. It came to a stop not fifty feet from the bus.

"Roger," answered Mike, glaring at the Iranian civilians.

"Mike," Joe whispered as he pushed past Mike. "Be careful and use restraint."

"Don't worry, buddy, I will," Mike answered with a grin.

Colonel Buckley quickly exited the plane, running toward the bus with several men from Delta Force. A second C-130 was circling, ready to land as Joe met his commanding officer on the ground outside the bus.

"What the hell is that bus doing here, Joe!" the colonel barked.

"It came down this deserted road, sir, just as you started your descent. There are forty-three civilian passengers, men, women, and children. There doesn't appear to be any military personnel or police on board. We searched them and found no weapons or radios. I'd like one or two other men guarding them to back up Sergeant Laurence," Joe reported.

"Marshall," Buckley called out to one of his men. "Put a couple of men on that bus." One of the men with him immediately ran off. "How about Desert Two?" he asked, returning his attention to Joe.

"Should be ready to go, sir. Staff Sergeant Ritchie and Sergeant Chavez have enough vehicles for all of us. The safe house near the embassy is prepped and ready."

"Well, at least that's going right. The sandstorm's put us behind schedule. Any signs of the helos?" he asked.

"No sir, you are the first one here," Joe replied. "Colonel, what are we going to do with the civilians?"

"We don't have much choice, do we? We have to take them with us. At least until this is all over; then we'll release them. The raid isn't until tomorrow and I don't think we can trust them not to tell their Uncle Khomeini, do you?" Colonel Buckley huffed.

"No, sir. We'll keep them on the bus until we're all loaded onto the helos. Then they can be loaded onto the C-130s."

"Now where are those damn helos?" Buckley bellowed.

Joe returned to the bus and stood outside with Mike. The night sky kept disappearing as the walls of sand washed over the makeshift desert airfield. At times the visibility was no more than five feet at best, making it incredibly dangerous for any aircraft to land. *It will truly be a miracle if they make it in this weather,* Mike thought, hoping the storm would blow over before the helicopters arrived. He struggled with Joe to keep their feet and cover their faces as the wind sandblasted them.

***

The storm was beginning to let up enough to let the aircraft head out to Desert Two closer to Tehran when Colonel Buckley was informed that a third helicopter had developed mechanical problems.

"There's no way that helicopter can make it, Colonel. Bluebird 2's hydraulic pump is shot. It's not safe to fly. If we don't want to scrub the mission, we have to go forward with only five helicopters," said the pilot and aircraft commander for the damaged helicopter.

Colonel Buckley now faced a serious dilemma. The mission plan was very clear: a minimum of six helicopters was required to successfully execute the dangerous mission. Fewer than that called for a mission abort. Buckley thought for a moment before replying.

"No way. I need six helos to carry all one hundred and twenty soldiers. And I need all the men I have to storm the embassy compound to rescue the hostages. Leaving out twenty shooters because we only have five helos will put the entire mission at risk. Besides, there's no guarantee more helicopters won't go down between here and Desert Two or, for that matter, to the extraction point in Tehran. The last thing I want to happen is for my men to be sitting in the middle of downtown Tehran with the entire city looking for them and no way out."

"So, we're aborting?" the pilot asked. At Buckley's nod, the senior pilot returned to his helicopter to begin destruction procedures.

"Damn," Buckley said out loud. "So close."

He looked at his watch, dreading the conversation he was now forced to have. He pulled out his satellite radio and called the operations center at the Pentagon where dozens of high-ranking men were following their every move on the ground. After Buckley's brief conversation with the task force commander, word was sent to the president for a decision.

"Yes, sir, I understand," Buckley replied into the radio a few minutes later. He had his answer.

"All right, mission's a scrub," he shouted to the team gathered around him. "Everyone get back on board the C-130s and prepare for takeoff. We're going home."

**

"What's going on, Joe?" Mike asked as his friend.

"I'm not sure. Something's not right. The men are getting back on the C-130s, not onto the helos. We're supposed to take the helos to Desert Two, not the aircraft."

"Change of plans?" asked Mike.

"I'll go check it out. Stay here with the bus."

"Great," Mike replied. "Want adventure? Join the Green Berets. You too can watch a bus!"

Joe grimaced at his friend, then made a beeline for Colonel Buckley, who stood between two C-130s barking orders. Just as he reached his boss, there was a huge explosion to his right. The blast sent Joe flying twenty feet. The soft sand broke his fall as he rolled to a stop. All sound left him, replaced only by an intense, monotonous ringing in his ears. He sat up, dazed as he looked up at the vision of hell before him. Bright flames rippled from one of the aircraft as the fuel it carried caught on fire. Intense heat seared his face.

As his senses returned, there were shouts and screams coming from all directions. Joe tried to get up, but sharp pain shot through his right shoulder. He looked down to see a piece of aircraft metal had cut into his flesh. Mike appeared and helped him up and away from the inferno.

"Damn, Joe, a helo crashed into the refueling aircraft as it was taking off!" Mike shouted. "I saw it. I saw you get thrown. Are you all right?"

"Yeah. I'm okay. It's not bleeding that much," he replied. "We got to get to the guys in the C-130. They're being burned alive."

Things got worse. More flames lit up the night sky as munitions went off inside the wreckage. Screams could be heard over the explosions, and the scent of charred flesh filled the nostrils of the Delta operators trying to reach their comrades in the burning aircraft.

Mike jumped on the rear ramp of the burning aircraft and plunged into the fiery coffin that was the fuselage. The burning bodies of his friends were strewn around him. He gagged on the smell of jet fuel mixed with charred flesh. He was astounded when Joe emerged from the smoky interior, hauling a badly burnt body as best he could, despite his own injury.

"There's no one left up in the front," Joe yelled as the scorching flames licked at their legs.

"No one's alive back here, either. Let's get out of here!" Mike yelled back, grabbing the unconscious pilot from Joe and slinging him onto his back.

The seconds seemed like hours as they made their way through the flaming hull, stumbling over the burned remains of their friends as they went. It was hard to breathe the searing air or see through the smoke, but finally they managed to get out.

Both men dropped to their knees and breathed deeply. Although the first breaths stung their burned lungs, the rush of cool, fresh air made Mike feel alive again. He rolled the pilot off his back and immediately started mouth-to-mouth. Joe jumped in to assist his friend by supplying lifesaving chest compressions. Together, they worked on resuscitating the man until the Delta medics arrived.

Exhausted, Joe and Mike leaned on one another in the sand, watching in a trance as the blazing aircraft, now a tomb for many of their friends, collapsed in on itself. One of the medics came over and bandaged Joe's arm as Colonel Buckley shouting orders for remaining aircraft to evacuate. He knew the explosion ensured that the Iranians would soon locate their position and send all they had to finish off the brazen Americans.

"Hey, let's go. Buckley said for everyone to bet on the planes. Let's move!" ordered a lieutenant colonel.

"I'm staying," Joe replied, staring as if mesmerized by the burning plane in front of him.

"Colonel Buckley said *everyone* was to evacuate. Now you two get on that plane!"

"Not this time. I've got men I still have to bring home," Joe said quietly. Bud and Hector would still be waiting at Desert Two, unaware of what had occurred due to the communications blackout. "Mike, get on that plane," Joe said.

"Nice try, old man. Let's go get our guys and get out of this hellhole . . . You know, Buckley's going to have our asses when he finds out we're not on that plane."

"No. He'll understand," Joe replied.

"What about them?" Mike asked, nodding at the frightened Iranian passengers staring wide-eyed out of the dirty windows of the old bus. Mike reached down and flicked the selector switch on his M-16 rifle from *Safe* to *Semi*.

Joe put a hand on his friend's firing arm. "No, Mike. You can't," he whispered, looking at a small girl huddled in her mother's lap, not much older than his own daughter, Lauren. "We're not going to kill them."

"Come on, Joe. You're jeopardizing the mission if you keep them alive."

"The mission is over."

"How about Bud and Hector? And us? You know every Iranian in the country will be searching for us if we let these people go and they tell what happened here. And they say that we didn't get on that plane. It's the only way for us to make it out of Iran alive, and you know it. It'll buy us the time we need to get to Desert Two, grab our guys and get the hell out of the country. You talk about reason and logic. This *is* the most logical course of action and you know it. You need to put your emotions aside, Joe, and face the facts," Mike persisted.

"Mike, if you murder these civilians in cold blood, you'll never forgive yourself. Maybe not today, but one day. It will haunt you for the rest of your life. Trust me, I know. We'll find another way," said Joe.

Mike lowered his weapon. "Damn it, Joe. You're going to get us all killed. For what? For these Iranians that want us dead anyway?"

"I'm not only doing it for them, Mike. I'm doing it for you. You'll thank me one day."

Mike just shook his head and walked off the bus.

Joe stared at the Iranians who had just escaped becoming victims in this war. He smiled at them, nodded, then walked over to the pickup truck the two Green Berets arrived in and took out some water and food. He returned to the bus and placed the supplies on the floor next to the front seat occupied by the driver. The driver nodded in apprehensive appreciation.

Joe took out his pistol and shot out the remaining three tires to fully disable the vehicle. As an added security measure, he popped the hood and pulled the spark plug cables from the engine, throwing them into the Toyota pickup along with the bus keys.

He then climbed into the passenger seat, knowing that the large fiery, explosion would soon bring the Iranian authorities, and the bus passengers would be rescued probably well before sunrise. "You drive," he said to Mike. "My shoulder hurts."

Mike swung up into the driver's seat. "Feel good about that?" he asked in a sarcastic tone, nodding to the bus as they drove past it. The little girl, he noticed, was staring at them through one of the windows.

"Yes. I do. And you will too one day."

"The way things are looking right now, I doubt we'll be alive tomorrow. And now we have a lot less water and food, since you gave it to the Iranians on the bus," he snapped. "What's the plan?"

"We go to Desert Two and pick up our guys. From there, we drive north into Turkey."

"Oh, just like that," asked Mike sarcastically.

"Yep, just like that. Just drive and drive fast. We need to get out of the country as soon as possible," Joe answered. "We have some time while the Iranians try to figure out what happened, but not much. Hopefully by then we will be over the border."

"I sure hope you know what you're doing," Mike muttered.

Joe sighed. "Me too."

Chapter Seventeen

MIKE LOOKED DOWN SADLY at his friend nearing death's door in this ICU room, far from the battlefields on which they had spent so many of their younger years.

"You dad was a hero, Lauren, both for bravery and decency. He was always the voice of caution and reason. He was so smart.

"In Iran, we all just wanted to go out and kick down doors and kill America's enemies. Joe was much more cautious. He was always focused on keeping us alive. He analyzed everything in nauseating detail, looking for any holes in any plan. It was actually very annoying. But his goal was always to successfully complete the mission with fewest casualties—on both sides. He knew we had no experience flying helos in the desert, especially at night. He also worried that Desert One could be compromised because of that road. He begged Colonel Buckley to get the Pentagon to modify some of the plans before the mission even got off the ground, but the brass wouldn't listen. Our ignorance and arrogance made us believe we were invincible. History proved us wrong. Your father proved us wrong.

"After we got back to Bragg, Joe told me that he thought if the mission wasn't aborted in the desert, our casualties would have been much higher when we assaulted the embassy in Tehran. I couldn't admit it then, but I knew he was right.

"That night Joe and I got drunk. Stayed drunk for a few days. That's when we got these tattoos, placed them over the burns on our arms that we got from rushing into the C-130 that night. We got them in memory of our friends lost in the Iranian desert. A lasting tribute to them. Not a day goes by where I don't think of them. And your father. He saved me that day. I don't know what would have happened if I had pulled the trigger on those innocent civilians. He saved something much more important than my life. He saved my soul. My conscience. My humanity.

"He was my sergeant, my mentor, but most importantly, he's my friend. That's why I told you some things here today I never should have. Classified things. I see the pain in your eyes. I know you struggle with your father's legacy. I want my friend's daughter to know just what kind of man he really is. Not just for all the things he's done for his country that you'll never know about. But for what he did for you."

Lauren stared at Mike, nearly breathless. "What? What do you mean, what he did for me?"

"He gave up his career to keep you safe."

"Safe? What do you mean by that?"

"I've talked long enough. Ask your mother," Mike said. He walked out of the ICU, leaving Lauren alone with her father. She sat there for several minutes, listening to the rhythmic beat of the monitors, digesting Mike's words, thinking about all the things her father had been through.

Nurse Maureen came in with an apology for disturbing her and started replacing the IV drip. Lauren mechanically said, "That's okay." When she stood to get out of the way, she realized she was stiff from sitting. She decided to take a walk to stretch her legs.

***

For a few minutes she walked aimlessly, until she found herself outside a small diner. The enticing smells emanating from the open door reminded her that it was lunchtime. She went in, sat at a table by the window, and ordered a bowl of homemade stew.

As she ate, she thought about her time with her father. When she was a little girl, she'd longed for his attention. He was her big, strong dad who would run around carrying her on his shoulders. He was strict about things, like bedtime and toothbrushing and being polite to one's elders, and he often told her how important it was to get a good education, to work hard at everything she did.

Then there had been the strange time, when he had come home on leave for several weeks. He'd been different. He spent a lot of time sleeping or just lying on the couch staring at nothing. She'd nearly forgotten about those days and how much it had worried her. *Why, it must have been after he got back from Iran,* she realized, connecting the dots. *And wasn't that when I broke my arm?* That memory was more vivid, at least, even though she was only in first grade.

She'd fallen out of a tree and broken one of the bones in her forearm. Her dad had picked her up and held her all the way to the hospital. And for a while after that he'd hardly let her out of his sight, walking her to and from school, listening to her tell him all about what she was learning. She'd reveled in his attention.

But it hadn't lasted. He'd gone back to work—overseas again— and was away when she had that really bad asthma attack, the one that landed her in the hospital for several days at age thirteen. He finally showed up the day before she got to go home again, but he left the day after that. She was so angry over his departure that she wouldn't say goodbye to him.

Then suddenly he was home again, announcing that he'd retired from the military and that they were moving to Hope. *If he'd come home for good earlier, it might have been different,* Lauren thought. But she'd been in the throes of early adolescence, all too ready to be critical of her parents. Plus, she was a true type-A personality, always driven.

When her dad asked her to come out into the garden to help him plant some flowers for her mother, Lauren would roll her eyes and go back to reading or studying. Yet, Lauren now realized she wanted him to be impressed with how hard she was working. *Talk about failure to communicate.*

"Need some more coffee, hon?" the waitress asked, shaking her out of the past.

"No, thanks. How much do I owe you?" Lauren asked, grabbing her small purse from off the table. "That stew was excellent, by the way."

"Oh thank you, hon. My grandmother's recipe. You don't owe me a penny."

"What?" Lauren asked, startled. "I haven't paid yet."

"No charge. You're Joe's girl, aren't you? I recognize you from the picture," the overweight, middle-aged woman said. Her hazel eyes were warm with a hint of sadness.

"What picture?"

"Your medical school graduation picture. Joe keeps it in his wallet. He showed it to me a while back, when he was in here taking a break from volunteering for something or another, can't remember what exactly. There's hardly a cause in this town your father's not involved with."

"You know my father?" Lauren asked.

"Hon, everyone knows your dad. He helps a lot of people out in these parts. Everyone's praying for him," she said. "You take care now." And she walked away to put the coffee pot back behind the counter.

Lauren finished her coffee in silence. She'd learned a lot about her father in the last twenty-four hours, but it seemed she was only scratching the surface. Still, she was perplexed. *Why? What was his motivation for his actions? Who is he, really? And can I save him?*

CHAPTER EIGHTEEN

LOST IN THOUGHT, SHE retraced her steps to the ICU. Her uncle was there again. "Hi, Uncle Harry," she said, giving him another hug, but her eyes were on her father's face.

"Hey, sweetie." Harry's sharp eyes took in her expression. "What is it?"

Lauren shook her head. "I need to talk to Mom. I thought she'd be here."

"She got a call and went home," Harry said.

"Okay. I'll go find her," Lauren said vaguely, and walked away again. She was aware that Harry said something about Chris as she left the room, but her mind was on what she had to ask her mother.

Audrey's car was in the driveway, but there was no sign of her in the house.

"Mom?" Lauren called out as she walked through the rooms. She was just about to go upstairs when she heard voices in the backyard and walked down the hall to the screened back door. There was her mother, sitting on a chair in the yard. She was talking to someone, but Lauren couldn't see who it was. As she pushed the screen door open, though, she heard a voice she knew well.

"What are you doing here?" she asked her estranged husband as she walked toward him.

Chris and Audrey broke off their conversation. Joey was running around the yard, kicking a soccer ball Joe kept for his grandson, but at the sound of her voice he yelled, "Hi, Mommy!" and ran up to her. As he hugged his mother with both arms, she was surprised by the wave of love that swept over her, washing away the brief flare of anger at Chris.

"Hey, baby. Oh, I have missed you," she said, sinking down to her knees and holding her son tightly.

"I missed you too, Mommy. Can we go see Poppy?" he asked, eyes wide with anticipation.

"Well, we'll see. You know Poppy's very sick. Sometimes when people are sick, they just need to rest and not be disturbed."

Audrey stepped up to them.

"Joey, go look in the side yard outside Nana's bedroom. Poppy put up birdhouses in all the trees so your Nana could hear the birds in the morning. I bet you can hear them singing if you're very quiet. Look for the blue ones."

Joey's face lit up and he ran off to the side of the house, looking for adventure.

"Chris, I thought we agreed you'd wait until I called you," Lauren said, watching the little boy run off.

"Yes, but when I didn't hear from you this morning as I expected, I decided to come anyway. Joey wants to see his grandfather, and like it or not I'm here, as his father, to help him do that."

His tone was unusually assertive, and Lauren bristled.

"Well, as his mother, I'm here to protect him from what could be a very traumatic experience."

"Now, Lauren," Audrey intervened. "Chris has rights too."

"Does he?" Lauren snapped, looking at her mother and then back at Chris. "Did you tell Mom about the papers you sent me?"

"Actually, we were just talking about that," he replied.

"Obviously you two have issues that need to be worked out," Audrey said. "Which you can only do by listening respectfully and openly to each other. That's hard at the best of times. The situation with your father is putting us all on edge, so I suggest that you put your marital problems to one side, at least for today, and focus on helping Joey understand what's going on with his poppy."

Lauren glared at her mother. *What a time to be playing counselor.*

"What are you saying? Are you suggesting I'm not open to working things out between us? I'm not the one who went to a lawyer and filed for divorce!"

Audrey put her hand on Lauren's arm, but dropped it as Lauren flinched away.

"You'll never get anywhere if you focus on blame. It's not about where things went wrong but about what is right with your relationship. Find the love you once had for each other and build upon that rather than pointing fingers at who did what wrong," Audrey said.

Lauren choked back the harsh words on the tip of her tongue. *It's not the time.*

"As you said, it's better we table this discussion right now." She looked pointedly at Chris. "Actually, Mom, I wanted to talk to you . . . Alone."

Chris got up and walked around the corner of the house, calling to Joey. Lauren could hear their voices. Joey seemed excited about the birds. She heard Chris say, "Sure, we can make a birdhouse," and the boy's enthusiastic cheer. *Chris always gets to be the one to say yes,* she thought. *Feels like I'm always the one saying no to Joey.*

"What is it, honey?" Audrey asked.

Lauren dragged her attention back to her question. "Mike Laurence told me about Tehran."

Audrey sighed. "Yes?"

"Mike told me about what happened to Dad in Iran. Then he said some things I didn't understand. About Dad and me. But he wouldn't explain. He said I should ask you."

Joey came running around the corner again and dashed up to Lauren. "Mommy, Daddy and I are going to make a birdhouse just like Poppy's and put it up so we can see the birds from the kitchen!"

"That's great, Joey," Lauren said, tousling his hair.

She looked up at Chris, who said, "Hey, little man. Nana and Mommy want to talk. Let's go inside."

"I don't want to go inside. I want to go see Poppy," the boy said, his mood switching from happiness to petulance.

Audrey got up and reached for Joey's hand. "Nana is going to see him now. Do you want to come with me?" Lauren glared. Now her mother was being defiant. *Why won't she answer my question?*

Audrey met her eyes and said softly, "You have a right to know. But right now, I just can't talk about it. Could you ask your aunt Joanna instead? She knows all about it." She looked from Lauren to Chris. "Is it okay for me to take Joey to see his poppy now?"

"I think that's a good idea. I'll follow you," Chris said.

Lauren opened her mouth to protest, but subsided, thinking, *Mom's a counselor. She'll know best how to help Joey deal with this. Better than me, at any rate. Time to be reasonable.*

"Joey, would you like to go with Nana?" she said. The little boy nodded. "Okay. Dad and I will be there soon."

***

Lauren and Chris watched Joey and Audrey walk hand in hand into the house. In a few minutes they heard a car start up and drive away. Lauren looked at her husband's worried face. All the fight drained out.

"Do you really want a divorce?" she asked quietly.

Chris looked down at the ground as if searching for the right words.

"I still love you, Lauren. But we've grown apart." He sighed, then looked at her. "Do you remember back in college, Lauren? We used to have such a good time. Sure, you studied a lot, but you still laughed when I teased you about being a nerd, and you'd put the books down for an hour to go out for a walk with me. We had fun. But we also had intimate moments where you opened up to me. That's what made me fall in love with you." He paused.

"For a long time, we made it work. Through medical school, even your residency when you came home only to sleep. Once you were hired on at Mass Gen, it got better. You were so happy to be doing what you were meant to do, and I liked my job, too. We took vacations—real ones. We had quality time together. And then we had Joey, and that was the best time of all." He looked away. "But in the last few years, you've become even more focused." He paused. "No, *obsessed* with your work."

"Chris, you have no idea the magnitude of my responsibilities at work. Peoples' lives are literally in my hands. I either do my job well, make no mistakes, or they die. Period. There are no second chances for mistakes. Why can't you understand that?"

"I do. I really do. But you take it to the extreme. Almost like you have to prove yourself to someone."

"Don't be ridiculous," Lauren said, but her voice faltered on the last word.

"Lauren, you aren't going to like hearing this, but I have come to think you're a bit insecure. Why else are you so driven to be the best doctor at the most prestigious hospital in the world?"

Her husband was asking the same question she'd asked herself earlier, but his tone put Lauren on the defensive. "Don't try to psychoanalyze me. It's called ambition. You might try it sometime."

Chris just looked at her. "That's not fair. We both agreed that I'd put my career on the back burner to take care of Joey. Something *you* were not willing to do."

"Don't lay that guilt trip on me. I love Joey more than anything. I would give up everything for him."

"Would you? Prove it." There was steel in his voice. Lauren gaped at him, not sure of what to say next. Chris waited a moment, then went on in a gentler voice.

"Do you know why I brought Joey here, even though you told me not to?"

"Why?"

"Back in Boston he said to me, 'Dad, whenever I visit Poppy, we tell each other a joke. He likes my jokes. It makes him laugh. Can we go see Poppy in the hospital? Maybe, if I tell him one of my jokes, it will make him laugh and he'll get all better.' He's so like you, Lauren. He wants to believe he can help everyone. But he can't. Just like you can't. I want Joey to understand that he's not always going to be in control. That it's not up to him to fix everything. That sometimes things just happen. I don't want him to be as hard on himself as you are on yourself."

Lauren looked down to hide the tears welling. *It's true. I can't fix them all, no matter how hard I try.*

Chris reached out and touched her hand softly. It startled her for a moment, but then she relaxed and allowed him to pull her into a hug. It felt wonderful. *When did we last hug?* She couldn't remember.

Chris said softly, into her hair, "I didn't mean to sound so harsh. I know my timing is bad. How are you holding up?"

Lauren shook her head against his chest. "I don't know. I've learned so much about my dad since I've been here. It's made me question everything I thought I knew about him. I mean, when I was little, I always thought of him as Mr. Tough Guy, the guy with all the rules. Then he came home and started planting gardens. I couldn't understand why. The big change. But now . . . I wonder if he was running from something."

"I don't know about that. *Running* may not be the right word. He's a pretty happy guy. Every time I've ever seen him, he was smiling and joking. He seemed content to me," Chris said.

"Well, yes, *now*. I mean, recently. But when he first came back . . . did you know he was a war hero? He's done some pretty hush-hush government things. He was doing important work. He was making a difference. Then suddenly he gives up his military career. He quits. Throws it all away and runs away to this little town. Away from a great career that he was successful at doing. Why? There's still so much I don't understand. Mom and Uncle Harry have been telling me some things, but I feel like something's being left out. I need someone who will tell me the full truth. I have to go talk to my aunt." She stepped away and looked at him. "Go on to the hospital. I'll see you there in a bit, okay?"

"Sure. Do what you need to do," Chris said gently and, for the first time in a long while, kissed his wife goodbye.

CHAPTER NINETEEN

THE TWO-STORY TUDOR STOOD on a large lot on Sycamore Place. Uncle Harry and Aunt Joanna's house was quite a bit larger than her parents' home, and the neighborhood was probably the nicest in the town. It might not be the typical lawyer's house one would find in Boston, but this wasn't Boston.

The door opened almost as soon as she rang the bell, to reveal a stylishly dressed, attractive woman, her graying hair pulled into a French roll.

"Lauren," said Aunt Joanna, smiling. "I missed you at the hospital earlier. I was just about to go looking for you." She hugged her niece. "Come on in. Harry just called. He's gone to court, but he'll be back at the hospital later."

Lauren returned the hug. She loved her aunt Joanna very much. Joanna had been the biology teacher at her high school and in many ways as much a mentor to her as Harry had been, encouraging her dreams of medical school. She and Harry had two sons, one practicing law in Philadelphia, the other in college at Stanford.

"How's your dad?" Joanna asked as they moved into the stylishly appointed living room, decorated in soothing neutrals that made a nice backdrop for several bold and colorful abstract paintings hung on the walls. Pictures of Harold Jr. and Isaac, Lauren's cousins, were displayed on a sideboard.

"Not well," Lauren replied sadly. "I'm trying to get a consult with a specialist at Mass Gen, but he's away today, so I have to wait to find out if there's anything more we can do. I hate waiting." As a doctor, waiting was always the hardest thing to do.

"It's just terrible," Joanna said, sitting on the couch and waving Lauren to an easy chair nearby. "Harry is so distraught. We all are. But if you're consulting a specialist, does that mean you think there's hope?"

"It's hard to say, Aunt Joanna. Sometimes people stay in comas for days or months. As for him getting better, well . . . it was a bad stroke. But you know I have to try everything."

A tear rolled down Joanna's cheek. "Of course you do. I saw your mother earlier. She seems to be holding up okay, but I worry about her. Joe's her rock."

"I know. I wish I could stay longer to be with her, but I really have to go back to Boston tomorrow, and I don't know when I can come back."

Joanna patted her hand. "You know we'll look after her here."

"I know you will, Aunt Joanna. But I'm feeling pulled in so many directions now, I hardly know where I am. Or who I am."

"I know one thing for sure. You're a very good doctor." Joanna smiled. "We're all so proud of you, Lauren."

"A whole lot of good that's doing Dad now."

"You can't think like that," Joanna admonished. "Sometimes, things just happen. It's nobody's fault and there's nothing anyone can do about it. Just you being here is a tremendous help to both your parents."

Is it? "It's so hard seeing him like this."

"I know. Your mom told me Chris and Joey were coming. Who knows, maybe Joey will be the miracle your father needs," Joanna said. "Joe loves him so much."

Lauren gave a noncommittal shrug. It seemed both Audrey and Joanna clung to the hope that Joey visiting his grandfather would actually make him better. *Well, haven't I been clinging to hope too? The bottom line is, none of us want to lose him.*

There was a long, pensive pause while Lauren wondered how to broach the topic of her father's traumatic experience.

"It's funny how life passes you by so quickly," Joanna mused. "One day you have lunch with someone, the next day he's in the ICU."

Lauren stayed silent, sensing her aunt was working up to something.

"It's made me think, Lauren. We waste so much time in our lives. We focus on work, school, money, but not on what's really important. So many of us never truly live our lives, we just punch the clock. Your father lived his life, though," she said with a smile. "Ever since he retired from the military and moved back here, he lived every day like it was his last. Do you know how hard it was to get Audrey away from that man just for us two to be able to go out for a girls' lunch? He wanted to spend every minute he could with her. Nothing else in the world mattered to him more than her. Except for you, of course. Harry and I love each other, but in terms of sheer devotion, we can't come close to Joe and Audrey. I don't know any couple that can."

"Well, not all couples can be as Disney-movie happy as Mom and Dad. Life has a way of becoming complicated for most of us."

"Life itself isn't complicated, Lauren. People make it complicated. There are choices people make and consequences of those choices and actions. You can choose to live happily, selflessly,

free from the restraints and pressures others impose on you, or you can blend into the herd. Life can control you, or you can control your life. It's all about choices." She paused for a moment.

"I probably shouldn't be telling you this, but your dad and mom had their share of problems, just like Harry and I have. Everyone does. The key is to work out the problems together. There should only be one side of a problem—the side you see together."

"Mom and Dad? They're the perfect couple," Lauren replied. "You just told me how much in love they still are."

Joanna gave her a measuring look. "You may not remember when they were having problems. You were so young."

There's my opening. "I don't remember, no, but I've just learned what happened to him in Iran."

Joanna blinked as if startled, then nodded. "Mike Laurence?"

"You know him, too?"

"Sure. He and your father are like brothers. As close as Joe and Harry."

"Well, he thought I should know," replied Lauren, still irked that she didn't recognize her own father's best friend.

"Then you probably know more than I do about what actually happened to him. All we knew is that he was with some secret military unit out of Fort Bragg, and that from time to time he'd go away. When he came back in 1980, he was . . . not himself."

Lauren nodded. "Please tell me about it. I want to know. Mom says I have the right to know, but she couldn't bring herself to tell me."

"I'm not surprised." Joanna took a breath. "Here's what I remember. Your father went away for a few months. He got hurt, but we didn't know how. Well, the physical wound wasn't very serious, although I remember thinking if Joe, as smart and careful as he always was, got hurt, he must have been in something bad. But the worst part was the psychological wound. He was clearly traumatized; he was sullen and withdrawn when he got back. From all of us, even Audrey. Harry said it had happened once before, after Joe got back from Vietnam, but that wasn't nearly as bad as this time." She sighed. "He started drinking . . . heavily."

"What?" Lauren asked incredulously. "I never saw him drink. I always thought Dad had no vices."

"It's true. Harry was terribly worried about him, remembering all the problems your grandfather had with alcohol." She looked at Lauren inquiringly. "Did you know about that?"

Lauren nodded. "Uncle Harry told me yesterday."

"Well, at least Joe was never mean or angry when he drank.

Never violent like your grandfather. He just became sad and distant."

"Sounds like he was self-medicating with the alcohol," Lauren commented. "Trying to numb the pain."

Her aunt nodded. "Probably. He withdrew into a different world. One far, far away. A world he wouldn't let any of us into. Not even your mother. Until you brought him back."

Lauren stared at her. "Me? What did I do?"

Her aunt nodded. "Joe told me the whole story later. It's time you heard it."

Chapter Twenty

Late Summer 1980, Fayetteville, North Carolina

EVERYTHING WAS DARK. THAT'S the only way he could describe it when he finally opened up to Joanna. His wife, his brother, they were too close. But his brother's new wife, a biologist, had more objectivity. She was a safe listener. Harry and Joanna had come down to visit. Despite Harry's claim that he had a legal conference in Raleigh for the week, Joe knew the couple had come down to North Carolina because Harry was worried about him and wanted to help his big brother.

After Iran, Joe tried to control the darkness that was slowly overtaking him, but he couldn't find the words to tell anyone or even help himself understand the depth of his darkness. He was just numb, emotionless. Nothing got through. No one could help.

The lack of sleep got to him. Nightmares were getting worse. He couldn't get the pictures out of his head. The screams. The smells. Now the vivid memories came to him while he was awake as well. He had seen plenty of death before, but this was different. His comrades' deaths were not only horribly painful and gruesome, they were caused by a preventable accident. It was a waste of good men that didn't have to happen.

He felt responsible. He'd seen the dangers. He should have been more forceful and insisted that the plan wouldn't work. His men had trusted him, and he had failed them.

Joe didn't know how to find peace with himself. The days dragged on, minute after painful minute, slowly, endlessly creeping by. He watched the clock as if obsessed, dreading the night. Not wanting to sleep. That's when it was the worst. That's when they came to visit him. Eight corpses, severely burned, all calling out his name. *Why?* they queried him nightly. *Why did you leave us to burn in the desert? We have no peace!*

Neither did Joe.

He spent his days moping around their small house in Fayetteville. Audrey was now a counselor on staff with the Cumberland County Health Department, working part time in the free mental health clinic downtown. But she was powerless to help her husband. No matter how hard she tried, she could not break Joe's depression. He wouldn't open up to her.

After the failed rescue attempt, Colonel Buckley gave the team some time off. Joe took an additional thirty days leave after that to try to sort out his feelings and put his life back together. The only thing that dulled the visions and pain was alcohol. As much as he knew he shouldn't drink, especially with his family history, it gave him temporary relief.

Audrey realized that something was seriously wrong with her husband as soon as he returned home. She had read the national newspapers, and it wasn't hard for her to figure out that Joe had somehow been involved with the events in Iran. She knew Joe couldn't tell her anything specific about the mission. But she couldn't get him to talk about it even in the most general terms.

It wasn't the fact that the mission was highly classified that tied Joe's tongue. It was his overwhelming guilt. He knew if anyone could help him, Audrey could. But he just couldn't tell her the truth about how he'd failed his friends.

Audrey wouldn't give up. "Joe, talk to me," she would plead when she found him sitting, head in his trembling hands.

"I can't," he would say, and walk out of the room if she persisted. "Just leave me alone!"

She persisted, even dragging him to see Dr. Stevens, the psychiatrist that Audrey worked for at the mental health clinic. He was a nice enough man, but he had never been in the military. He certainly didn't have experience with special operations. Joe had walked out halfway through the first session.

When Audrey came running after him, he'd said only, "Audrey, I need time to sort this out. Just give me that, okay?" and walked off. She acquiesced, although it hurt her. Audrey, who wanted nothing more than to help everyone, couldn't help her own husband.

Some days Joe walked the streets for hours until the bars opened. He'd stop in one after the other, trying to drown his pain. He wasn't alone. In many of the bars around the heavily Army-populated town of Fayetteville, scores of young vets sought solace from their demons. Joe sat with them quietly, nursing his drinks. One by one, they would leave. Joe wondered if they found any resolution or absolution in the cold bar or if they were still as empty as he was.

No matter how late it was when he came home, Audrey would be waiting up for him. "Why? Why, Joe?" she would ask. "Why won't you let me in?" Joe said nothing. The pain he was causing her only increased his guilt. In tears, Audrey would go to their bedroom. Most nights, Joe passed out on the couch.

One morning, Joe heard something that resembled a bell resounding in his hungover and aching brain. The light shining in through the windows didn't help. Then he heard the sweet sound of Audrey's voice. He opened one eye enough to see her talking on the phone.

"I'll be there as soon as I can. You hold on, now. Can you do that?" she asked. Even in his hungover state, Joe could hear the concern in her voice. He lifted his head.

"Oh good, you're awake," Audrey said as she hung up. "Joe, I just got a call from work. One of my clients is waiting for me at the clinic. He's suicidal, Joe, and I have to go. I've called Joanna to come pick Lauren up. Harry's at the conference, but she'll jump in the rental car and come down. It'll be a good half hour before she gets here. Can you manage with Lauren until Joanna arrives? She's still asleep."

"Go ahead, I'll watch her," he said softly, putting his head back down on the couch and closing his eyes. He was aware that Audrey was still standing there, as if indecisive. *Doesn't trust me*, he thought. *That's right. I fail people.* But then he heard the door shut and knew she had left the house.

As he lay there, head spinning, the visions crept back into his head. That's what bothered him the most; they came whenever they wanted. The faces, the cries, the smell of the charred flesh, as real as it was on that fateful night months ago. He tried to get up, but he couldn't get his balance. The alcohol still in his system made him weak and confused. He staggered a bit, then got down on his hands and knees to steady himself. *Why is this happening to me?* he thought tearfully, lying on the floor. The pain was too much for him to bear. Every night they haunted him. *Why won't it go away? Why won't they go away?* Then he felt a familiar object pressing on his chin. *If I ever needed St. Jude, now's the time*, he thought, grasping the cool medal around his neck and praying hard, the tears flowing fully now.

"Daddy," a voice said, startling him.

Joe looked up to see his daughter standing in front of him. She looked like an angel, just like her mother had looked to him the first time he saw her. Little Lauren put a cool cloth on her father's forehead and smiled.

"Hey, Rennie. What are you doing?" Joe managed with a forced smile.

"I'm making you better, Daddy," the little girl answered. "You're sick, but I'm a doctor and I'll make you better," she assured him confidently, placing her plastic toy stethoscope on her father's chest.

Then she turned and went into the kitchen, returning with a small package. "Here, Daddy, take this medicine," Lauren ordered, handing her father a handful of M&M candies. "It'll make you better."

The hard shell around Joe's heart cracked. The idea of eating nauseated him, but he swallowed the candies to please her.

"Thank you, honey. I feel better now. I just need to lie down a little longer."

Joe lay back on the rug and shut his eyes. *Just another minute. Then I'll get up.* "That's okay, Daddy. You lie down," Lauren answered, placing the cool cloth on her father's forehead.

The scream woke him from an uneasy dream. Trained reflexes kicked in, and Joe was on his feet, wide awake and looking around him for any danger. The scream came again, and then he heard Lauren calling out for him from the yard. He ran outside to see a sight worse than any of his nightmares—his little girl lying on the ground under a tree, her face twisted with pain.

Hours later, Joe sat on the same couch in the living room, still wracked with guilt. Joanna had arrived just as Joe reached Lauren. Lauren had broken her left forearm. Joanna drove them to the hospital, then called Audrey while Joe stayed with his daughter. Audrey arrived in time to hold Lauren's right hand while the doctor applied the cast, Joe still holding his daughter tightly in his strong arms. She hadn't rebuked Joe, but Joe felt like a whipped dog anyway. Joanna drove him home while Audrey remained at the hospital with Lauren as the two waited for pain meds at the pharmacy.

"What have I done?" Joe asked Joanna in the car as they drove the short distance to their base housing unit. He had opened up to her about his nightmares and depression.

"Joe, I know you've been through a lot since you've been in the military. Harry's told me a little about what you two experienced in Vietnam. I can't even imagine what you've done since joining Special Forces. But, whatever it is, you've got to get past it," Joanna said. "Use all that strength, discipline and willpower that I know you have to overcome this and get on with living your life. If not for you, for Audrey and Lauren."

Joe listened quietly, agreeing.

"You determine your fate," she continued. "You can control what's going on inside you. Don't let the pain and darkness win, Joe."

Despite her insistence that she wait with him until Audrey and Lauren arrived home, Joe convinced Joanna that he'd be all right. In fact, he said he preferred to be alone to think things over.

"I've got to get past this. I can't let the past come between me and my family. I can't hurt them again. I have to move on. This is it," he said aloud to the empty house. "Just like Joanna said, I have the ability to control this. Life is for the living, and I'm going to start living today."

Joe took a shower and shaved for the first time in a week. When he came downstairs, Audrey was sitting at the table. Joe noticed her hands were shaking and her eyes were bloodshot from crying.

"Lauren's asleep," she said. She looked at him. It seemed to him she was steeling herself to say something, and he feared he knew what it might be. *We can't go on like this.*

He had to speak first. He knelt down by her and took her hands.

"I'm so sorry for the way I've been acting. First, I need to say that, truth be told, if it wasn't for you and Rennie, I would probably be dead by now. Nothing in my world is more important than you two. I realized that today. All the pain I've been in pales in comparison to the pain I felt when I saw Lauren lying there, hurt. Because of me. It was my fault. It was because I was too hungover to watch over her. Wallowing in my own self-pity and grief. That will never happen again, I swear. I've taken my last drink."

"Oh, Joe," Audrey said, seeing the resolve in her husband's eyes, knowing the old Joe was back. "I was so worried about you. I know something bad happened to you. I just want to help you through it."

"I know. And I'm ready to tell you about it now."

***

Joanna picked up a tissue, dabbed her eyes and handed another to Lauren. She composed herself, and took a deep breath.

"That morning, your father told your mom all that had happened overseas and about the torment he was going through. Audrey finally got him to see Dr. Stevens and, after a long time in therapy, he came out of it. For the most part, anyway. As much as anyone could ever recover from the horrors of war." Joanna sighed.

"It wasn't easy for either of your parents. You know that post-traumatic stress and depression don't just affect the victim. The families have a hard time, as well. That experience is why Audrey went back to school and got her master's degree. She was already an expert in PTSD, in a way, and she wanted to turn that to good use."

"Dad had a nervous breakdown; is that what you're telling me?"

"No, that's not it at all. He was just going through a hard time. You know, there are a lot of people like Joe who are strong enough to help others, to run to their aid, do what they can to ease their pain. But they don't always know how to take care of themselves. He was too proud to get help and couldn't pull himself out of his depression on his own. It was his love for you, Lauren, that brought him out of his deep abyss. It was the pain he saw he was causing you and your mother that allowed him to lift the shroud of darkness that had come over him and see clearly again. It wasn't over that day, but he put himself on the path of recovery. From that moment on, he never took another drink. And over time, he started to come to terms with his past."

Lauren sat quietly, thinking back. She did have a vague memory of her father being sick and making him better. *Maybe that's why I decided to be a doctor,* she realized. *Because of my dad.*

Chapter Twenty-One

WHEN LAUREN WALKED INTO the ICU later that afternoon, the young nurse she had mistreated the night she arrived was on duty. The nurse tensed when Lauren approached.

"Listen," Lauren said, "I'm sorry about the way I spoke to you the other night. I was wrong. I'd like to say it was because I was upset about my father's condition or give you another excuse. But the truth of the matter is, sometimes I can be a real jerk. You didn't deserve the way I acted toward you and it won't happen again. Thank you for taking such good care of my father."

The nurse gasped and then composed herself.

"Oh, that's all right. I understand." When Lauren didn't move away, she went on, "I'm so sorry about your father. I would do anything for him. My brother worked for him for a while. No one else would hire him because he had a police record. He was going through a rough time, not knowing what to do with his life after high school and got in with the wrong crowd. Not only did your father give him a job and mentor him, but he pulled some strings for Pete to get into a community college. I guess your father did some landscaping for the college dean and he was his friend.

"Pete ended up putting his life together, went on to get a bachelor's degree in engineering, and now he's doing well in Manhattan, has a good job and is engaged to a nice woman he met at work." She grinned. "Pete's not a bad guy. He was just young and immature at the time. He did his time and all he needed was a second chance. Your dad was one of the few people that saw the good in my brother, and he was able to get through to him."

"What a nice story. Thank you for sharing . . . Beth," Lauren said, noting the embroidered name on the nurse's uniform. *Is there anyone in this town who Joe Keller hasn't helped?* "I'm glad everything worked out for Pete. Is Dr. Spiva on the floor?"

"Oh, he should be here shortly. He usually makes his afternoon rounds in about a half hour or so." She paused. "Your family's all gone down to the cafeteria. Was that your son with them? He's adorable."

"Joey, yes."

"He was hungry, so they took him to get something to eat."

Lauren nodded. *He's eating, so I guess Joey's handling seeing his grandfather like this*, she thought as she entered Joe's room. Once again, Lauren checked her father's vital signs and performed a quick neurologic exam. No change, except for some slight signs of mottling on his legs, which could mean he was going deeper into coma. Suddenly aware that she was exhausted, she sat, closed her eyes and waited for Dr. Spiva.

Monitor alarms startled Lauren awake. Somehow, she had ended up lying with her head on the bed, holding Joe's hand. She jumped up to see what was wrong with the patient and realized the alarms were coming from another room. Her father's condition was unchanged, but she noticed an unmistakable aroma in the air. On the metal stand near the bed sat a tall cup of coffee, emitting the unique scent of French vanilla. There was a yellow sticky note beside the cup that read: *From me and Pete. Our prayers are with you, your father and your family. B.*

She took a sip of the steaming brew. Just what she needed. She stretched her arms high into the air, then strolled out of the ICU room and walked up the nurses' station, where Beth was going over notes and patients' charts with a small team of nurses who, Lauren surmised, must have been the evening shift. Despite her apparent youth, Beth sounded surprisingly competent. Lauren fought the urge to interrupt, waiting patiently at the counter as she sipped the coffee, which was unexpectedly good for hospital fare. Finally, Beth was free and turned to her.

"Dr. Keller? How can I help?"

"Call me Lauren, please, Beth. Has Dr. Spiva arrived yet?"

Beth nodded. "I believe he's up on the pediatric ward. Go out to the lobby and take the elevator up to the second floor . . . Lauren."

"Thank you," Lauren said with a tired smile. "And thank Pete for the coffee," she said.

Lauren left the ICU. But instead of taking the elevator, she headed up the stairs to the pediatric ward. The effort helped her wake up. She reached the second floor and entered the ward. There were six rooms in the hall, with a small nursing station in the middle. Lauren spotted Dr. Spiva about to go into a patient's room. She called out to him and hurried to his side. He looked up and smiled as she approached. Then his smile faded.

"I suppose you did a neuro check on your father? Did you notice any changes?"

"How did you know I was there?"

"I know everything that goes on in my hospital, Lauren. Patients, their families, and staff. Don't you?"

Lauren was taken aback. She prided herself on knowing everything about her patients' conditions, but she knew almost nothing about who they were, their lives, their families. *Most of the time I barely know their names*, she thought, remembering how Faye Sutton had corrected her on the pronunciation of Mr. Szary's name. Her residents took care of the day-to-day management of her patients, while she made all the medical decisions during rounds and in conferences. On a good day, she would maybe spend five or ten minutes with each patient.

"Apparently not as well as you do," she humbly replied.

"It's one advantage of working in a small hospital. There are others. Come, round with me, Doctor," Dr. Spiva invited as he led Lauren into his patient's room. There was an eight-year-old girl in the bed. A young woman, no doubt her mother, sat beside the girl with a book in her hand.

"Hi, Suzy," Doug said with a smile as he walked up to the hospital bed. "Hi, Pat," he said to the mother. "This is Dr. Lauren. She's helping me today."

"Dr. Doug!" the little girl snapped with a smile.

"Well, missy, I hear you've been up and about, running down the halls, driving the nurses crazy," Dr. Spiva remarked as he tapped her nose playfully.

Suzy chuckled, glancing mischievously at her mother.

"She must be better. That's just how she is at home too," her mother said, smiling back at the child.

"Suzy, do you want to go home today?" Dr. Spiva asked.

"Yay! Can I take these with me?" she asked, pointing to some of the toys and stuffed animals scattered on the bed.

"No, they belong here for all the kids to play with. But I got you a better one," Dr. Spiva said, pulling a doctor Barbie from the pocket of his long white doctor's coat.

The little girl grabbed the doll. "Mommy," Suzy exclaimed, "now I can be a doctor, too!"

"You bet you can. You can be anything you want to be. Now, your first job as a doctor is to take care of yourself and try not to get sick again. The best way to do that is to eat all the food your mother puts on your plate, and go to bed when she tells you to. Can I count on you, Dr. Suzy?" Dr. Spiva asked.

"Yes, sir," Suzy replied, bouncing in the bed.

"Thank you, Doctor, for everything," Suzy's mom said warmly.

"You're welcome, Pat. I'll have some antibiotics and Tylenol in the pharmacy downstairs for you to pick up when you leave. Why don't you bring her by my office tomorrow, say around lunchtime, just for me to take a peek at her? Remember, if she starts throwing up again or if you have any concerns at all, just call me anytime. You have my home and cell number."

"I will, and thanks. Here, I baked these cookies for you. Chocolate chip, your favorite. There were a dozen cookies in the tin, but you-know-who got to them about a half hour ago," Pat said, nodding to Suzy.

Suzy smiled broadly and shrugged.

"Suzy, I'll share my cookies with you anytime," Dr. Spiva said with a wink, taking the not-quite-full tin from her. "Thanks a bunch, Pat. The nurse will be in with the discharge papers in a moment. I'll see you tomorrow."

Lauren followed Dr. Spiva out of the room.

"Are you crazy? You gave her your home and cell numbers," she exclaimed. "I'd never dare to do that. I'd be hearing from the hypochondriacs all day and night!"

Dr. Spiva chuckled. "Well, maybe in a big city with all those people. But practicing medicine in a small town where you know everyone is different. Sure, I have a couple of patients who call me over every little thing. But most of my patients respect my time and only call if they're sincerely worried. Cookie?" He opened the tin. The smell of a fresh-baked chocolate chip cookie was irresistible. It was still warm and tasted just like the ones Lauren's grandmother used to bake for her.

Dr. Spiva took a cookie too, then put the tin on the counter at the nurses' station for all to enjoy.

"Suzy is the third generation in her family that I've had the privilege to care for. I delivered Pat thirty-one years ago, and I still care for her parents. They're actually dear friends of mine. And your father's, I might add. I delivered Suzy as well. It was a tough delivery," he said, staring off into the distance. "A long, cold December night. I had to use forceps to get little Suzy out. She was stubborn then and just as stubborn now. That's probably how she pulled through her bad pneumonia this week."

He looked at Lauren. "They trust me and depend on me. And I trust them, too. We're partners in their health care. That's why I'll always be available to my patients whenever they need me. To me, that's the difference between a physician and a doctor."

Lauren suddenly saw the old man standing before her in a new light. She had worked with some of the most brilliant and talented physicians in the world. But standing before her was truly a gifted healer. No wonder her father had placed so much faith in him. Doug reminded her of her own mentor back in Boston, Carl Russell.

"Come, Lauren. There's one more thing you need to see." Lauren obediently walked with him out of the ward. She felt like she was back in her own training days, following yet another teacher to learn from his wisdom.

However, she was unprepared for what she saw next. As they turned the next hall, Lauren's jaw dropped. *The Lauren A. Keller Children's Asthma Center* was printed in large letters above the double door.

She shot a bewildered look at Doug, who gave her a huge grin.

"Believe it or not, this little hospital has the only dedicated children's asthma center this side of Philadelphia," Doug said proudly, ushering Lauren through the doors. Inside was a state-of-the-art clinic complete with a small ward and pulmonary diagnostic center. "We have three pulmonologists and one of the best allergists around on staff," Doug told her. "We get referrals from all across eastern Pennsylvania."

"But why is *my* name over the door?"

"Do you remember when you were hospitalized for that bad asthma attack when you were thirteen years old?"

"Sure. Mom and I were in DC. Dad was overseas."

"Yes. Your father was spending a lot of time in the Middle East after those Marines were killed in that awful bombing in Beirut." Doug paused. "But as you well know, the DC area is not the best place for asthmatics; they don't call it 'Foggy Bottom' for nothing."

Lauren nodded.

"Your asthma got worse the first two springs you were there when the trees started to bloom, but stayed manageable with inhalers and, at times, breathing treatments. However, that year you had a huge flare-up, much worse than usual. Your regular doctors had a hard time getting it under control. Your mother called me in a panic. I'd been chief resident at Johns Hopkins some years prior and I pulled a few strings to get you admitted there. Your bronchi were so clamped down you had to be intubated. You had us all scared to death," Doug told her.

Lauren thought back. Most of that memory was a blur, but she had a sudden recollection of being in a hospital bed, looking up at her father's worried face.

"Dad came home," she said.

"Yes, Joe was away overseas on some secret mission. But he took emergency leave and came home as soon as he found out you were in the hospital," Dr. Spiva confirmed. "Would you like me to tell you the whole story?"

More revelations, Lauren thought. She nodded. "I would. But first, I think I need a chair. And another cookie."

Chapter Twenty-Two

March 1987, Johns Hopkins Medical Center,

Baltimore, Maryland

JOE SAT CLOSE TO Lauren's bed. He had only been home for a day, and they were already calling him to return to the Persian Gulf. He had been working throughout the Middle East for the last few years after moving his young family to Washington DC in 1984. First, he'd been attached to a clandestine paramilitary group out of CIA headquarters in Langley, Virginia, collecting intelligence on the terrorists that blew up the Marine barracks in Beirut. This work was very different from the work he had been doing at Fort Bragg. There were no late-night raids on houses or hostage rescues. After the Beirut bombing, Joe worked as a handler, running a dozen or so sympathetic Lebanese who were giving him information on the Islamic Jihad terrorists operating in the region.

But then the Iran-Iraq war heated up, and Joe was sent to the Persian Gulf to help protect American-flagged vessels. Oil tankers were being attacked by Iranian patrol boats. Joe had been sent to a secret base on a converted oil platform in international waters to help protect the flow of oil through the Straits of Hormuz. The work was intriguing, but as soon he found out Lauren had been admitted for a severe asthma attack, he couldn't focus. After much insisting from Joe, his boss allowed him to fly home, but only for three days.

He stroked his daughter's long blonde hair, holding back tears. Lauren had been intubated for two days now. Her asthma exacerbation was one of the worst the doctors had ever seen. Since her transfer to Johns Hopkins, the hospital staff had bent over backwards for the Keller family.

One reason for the preferred treatment was Dr. Doug Spiva, who came down from Hope to be with Joe, Audrey and their baby girl. Dr. Spiva still had connections at Johns Hopkins. Also at the family's side was Mike Laurence consoling his best friend.

Audrey had been beside herself, close to a nervous breakdown at the sight of her baby with a tube down her throat. She was now asleep on the other bed in the room; Dr. Spiva had given Audrey some medication to help her rest and quiet her nerves.

"I've decided not to join Operations when I retire," Joe said abruptly, referring to the Directorate of Operations at the Central Intelligence Agency.

"What? But you've wanted to work with the CIA for years. What's happened?" Mike asked, surprised.

Joe sat pensively, staring at his daughter. "Mike, you've said many times you'll die in uniform. And you know, after we came back from Iran, I believed I could do more good on the intelligence-gathering and analysis side of the house rather than being a straight trigger-puller with Delta. I wanted to find the bad guys *before* they acted, so the government could respond before anyone got hurt. I thought that the CIA would put me in a better position to do that than the military."

"Yeah, I know. I know you weren't truly happy at Delta. And I've always thought your intelligence—no pun intended—would be better used at the CIA than in the military. But now you want to throw all those dreams away? Listen, I know it's hard seeing your little girl in the hospital like this. But she will get better. Don't make any rash decisions now. Give it some time and think about it," Mike pleaded.

"I have been thinking about it. Ever since Iran," Joe replied. "Audrey and I have discussed it and I made my decision. I just don't want to be away from my family anymore. Besides, there's no way my family can continue to live anywhere near Langley. The pollen is so bad in Northern Virginia and DC; Lauren's health would suffer. She'd be in the hospital with one asthma exacerbation after another," Joe said. "While I would be deployed to some hellhole somewhere, fighting a bureaucracy trying to get a few days off to be with my sick daughter."

"Think of all the reasons you wanted to join the CIA. You're smart, Joe. Too smart for the Army. You can do so much more."

Joe shook his head. "I almost lost her, Mike. It's made me think about what really matters in life."

"Stopping terrorism, that doesn't matter?"

"Sure it does," Joe countered. "But I've done what I can. I've done my time. Someone else can go on with that work." He looked soberly at the younger man. "After Iran, I vowed to Audrey that I'll never bring harm to our family again. I won't risk Lauren's asthma getting worse living here. When you and Becky have children, you'll understand. I've hurt them enough the way it is. I've been gone so much. Over the past few years, I could tell that my relationship with Lauren is suffering. She's growing up. She'll be gone soon, out of the house and away at college somewhere. I need to be there for her while I can," he finished.

"What will you do?" asked Mike.

"After my mom passed away a few years ago, I haven't had the time or, quite frankly, the heart to sell her house. It's just sitting empty back in Hope. Lauren seemed to do better up there in the mountains when we'd go visit. Next year I'll have completed my twenty years. I can retire then. Maybe we'll move back to Hope, and I'll do something."

"What?" Mike asked. "What could you possibly do in rural Pennsylvania after being in Special Forces? You'll go stir crazy."

Joe smiled at his old friend. "I'm not like you, Mike. I never liked many aspects of our job. I won't miss it. Maybe I'll do something completely different. We've spent so much time destroying lives. Maybe I'll try to make people's lives better."

"Don't get philosophical on me, Joe. We did what we had to do in order to save American lives. The hits we made were on people who deserved it. And you were always the one who went the extra mile to ensure no civilians got hurt."

"That might be true, but that doesn't alleviate my conscience any. I'm not saying what we did wasn't necessary. I'm just saying I won't do it at the cost of my family anymore."

"Alright," Mike said. "I'll help anyway I can, you know that. But I think you're making a mistake."

"I know you do. But I'm sure I'm not. I appreciate your support, as always. You're a good friend, Mike." Joe looked back at his daughter and took her hand.

"Remember, Lauren may be your daughter, but she's my namesake. She's tough as nails and she'll pull through this just fine," Mike said. "Right, Doc?"

Dr. Spiva had been listening silently to this exchange. He looked up and said, "Yes, I'm sure she will. But Joe's right. Air quality, pollen counts, temperature, elevations, even smoking laws, all can make an area more problematic and even dangerous for people with breathing problems. This area seems to have a perfect storm of environmental factors that can contribute to more hospitalizations for asthmatics."

"Thanks, Doug," Joe replied. He bent his head down and took his medal off from around his neck, then clasped it around his daughter's neck. "Help her, St. Jude. Please," whispered Joe. He stood. "I need to make the call to Langley to let them know my decision."

Joe walked off and Mike and Doug remained. Audrey was still sleeping peacefully.

"You know," Mike said softly to Doug, "I've been with Joe most of my adult life. Joe's been my mentor, a big brother and a friend. I've always had Joe there to guide me. I'm not sure what I'll do, now that he's retiring from the military."

"Maybe it's time for you to show him that he taught you well. Live his legacy," the family doctor said.

Mike grunted. "It's funny you should say that. For years, our commanding officer has pushed us both to put in officer packages. Joe refused; he always felt the closer he was to his men, the more he could do to protect them. I just wanted to work with Joe. But maybe now . . . maybe I will."

***

Later that night, Doug sat with Audrey in the garden outside the hospital. She had awoken to news that Lauren's condition was improving. The tube was out, and she was breathing okay on her own. Mike left to get takeout for them all. Joe still held vigil over Lauren. Meanwhile, Dr. Spiva talked Audrey into taking a brief walk outdoors.

"Did Joe tell you he's going to put in his retirement papers?" Audrey asked. "He wants us all to move back to Hope."

"I think that's great news," Dr. Spiva responded. "But what do you think?"

"I really don't know. I've always believed that Joe was happy at work most of the time, although I know he was troubled by some of the things he did."

"Something happened in Iran," Dr. Spiva said. "I've picked that much up."

"Yes." Audrey looked suddenly very sad. "I thought he was over it. But now I know he's been suffering for years. He's looking like he did when he came back from Iran. He's tired. He told me last night that his work has been steadily taking a toll on him, chipping away at his soul little by little. All the war zones he's deployed to. He said to me, 'People fighting and killing each other, for what? Power?

Money? Prestige? They may say it's about religion or land or pride, but in the end, it was always a few people in power that cause misery for millions over things that really don't matter much in life.' He was done. He'd seen too much death."

Dr. Spiva nodded. "Would you be happy in Hope?" he asked. "All of you?"

"I'll be happy if Joe is happy," Audrey said. "I'll finish my master's in counseling psychology next month, and I can find work anywhere we go. But will Joe be happy? I asked him, how will he feel when he hears that an American somewhere was taken hostage or, God forbid, we get into another war? I asked him what he'll do if his friends get sent into harm's way again and he won't be there to save them." She looked up at the night sky. "Do you know what he said? He said, 'I'll pray for them. I'll pray for all sides to see reason and not butcher each other. In the meantime, I'll do what I can to make this world a better place, starting with a better life for you and Lauren.'" She wiped at her eyes.

"Sounds like his mind is made up."

Audrey nodded. "I could change it. I could talk him out of this decision, I'm pretty sure. And if I felt he really wanted to work for the CIA, I would. But I don't. Year after year, he's become more and more introspective, less interactive, more pensive and withdrawn. He needs to find his peace before it's too late. I intend to see tha he does."

"And Lauren? How will she feel about the move?"

"That's the problem," Audrey admitted. "I suspect that Lauren will hate to leave DC. She loves the museums, libraries, and historical sites. Like many young people, she prefers a big city to a small town.

"The really tricky part is that Joe doesn't want Lauren to know why we're leaving. He thinks she'll blame herself for him retiring from a job she thinks he loves and that we're moving for her. He doesn't want her carrying that baggage with her the rest of her life. So, he doesn't want to tell her the truth."

"I'm not sure that's wise," Dr. Spiva said. "If she loves the city so much and she's uprooted without an explanation, won't she blame Joe? You know how adolescents can sometimes unreasonably blame their parents for everything."

"I know, but Lauren has missed her father so much, maybe having him back full time will balance that out. I'm hoping what Joe hopes, that they'll get back their old, close relationship in Hope." She stood up.

Doug stood and walked with her. "I hope you're right. So, what do you think Joe will do for a job in Hope, Pennsylvania?"

Audrey laughed. "You won't believe it."

"Try me," the doctor said, smiling.

"We were sitting out here earlier and he was telling me that, although all those deserts he had deployed to had their own beauty, he thought that maybe if there were more flowers and gardens, people would be more relaxed and calm. He said to me, 'That's what I'll do. I'll plant plants.' He's going to become a gardener."

"Joe the gardener," Dr. Spiva mused, trying to picture the career Army man in that role. "This I gotta see."

"Well, you will," Audrey replied as they entered the hospital. "He said to me, 'Think about how happy you are when you see a beautiful garden. What do people do when it's a nice, sunny day? They go to the park, or out into their yard with their families. They play ball in the field or roll in the grass. Flowers, plants, trees and nature all make us happy, calm. At peace.' I could hear it in his voice, Doug. He's found a new passion. I think he'll be wonderful at it."

"So, you're really moving to Hope."

"Yep. The mortgage is all paid off. Joe's pension will hold us over nicely until we can get our new careers going." She laughed. "I made him promise me one thing. I told him, 'You'd just better make me the best garden on the block, or else.'"

CHAPTER TWENTY-THREE

LAUREN SAT, DIGESTING THIS new insight into her past. It was uncanny—amazing really—that she had so little recollection of her asthma ever being that severe. But with the powerful drugs used to keep a patient sedated while intubated, she wasn't completely surprised that she had blocked much of that experience out of her memory. She did recall having a lot of nasal congestion as a kid and, on occasion, feeling short of breath especially when being active outdoors. Perhaps one reason she stayed indoors so often to read wasn't because she was antisocial. *Maybe it was because I simply felt better.*

"So, we moved to Hope because of my asthma," Lauren said. *My dad wasn't oblivious to my needs after all. He was protecting me.*

"Yes." The older doctor nodded. "About five years ago, Joe came to my office one day and said he wanted to ask a favor. Now, your father rarely asked anyone for anything. He was a giver, not a taker. Of course, I said yes, but I was shocked at what he considered a *favor*. He asked me if I could set up a children's asthma center in Hope to help keep kids from going through what you went through. For someone with no medical experience, he was surprisingly specific. He wanted it to focus on research, prevention, and treatment. I told him it could be done, but it would be expensive. He only nodded and handed me a check for several thousand dollars, then told me, 'I'll make sure you get the rest of what you need.'"

"How did he do that? He didn't have that much money, certainly not from an Army pension and small landscaping business."

Doug laughed. "Well, he did it. He went all over town asking individuals, businesses, anyone he could reach, to donate. He approached corporations to donate the equipment. I think that's how he got the initial money. I believe Audrey also helped him apply for a grant. But most of the major long-term support, resources and funding came after Joe enlisted the help of an old friend of his from the Army. Hector Chavez is a state senator down in Philly. Been in office for decades now. He's been a big support of our program for those decades.

"After Joe got him involved, a number of charitable organizations and state resources poured in to help make the Center what it is today. Temple University has even teamed up with us to study the effects of weather on asthma. A lot of exciting work is being done out of this small but impressive center." Doug looked pensive. "You know, I asked him once why he wanted to do this. He looked down at the floor and quietly uttered one word: 'penance.'

"I still don't know why he felt he had to redeem himself. Maybe it was from all the things he did in the military; maybe it was for his guilt that he let you down, putting you in a position where you got sick. Maybe for not being there for you all those years he was overseas. Regardless of the reasons, the clinic opened several years later, just after you went off to college.

"Your mother and I pushed him to invite you to attend the grand opening of the clinic, but he resisted. I wish you could have been there the first time he saw what his love for you had created. His eyes were filled with tears when he was told what great work the clinic would do for young asthmatics. I'll never forget the words he said to me when he saw the original sign. He said, 'Thanks, Doug, the clinic's perfect. There's only one thing wrong.'

"'What?' I asked him. He pointed to the plaque that had his and Audrey's name on it. 'The plaque's wrong. Take it down,' he told me. 'It was *Lauren* who made this possible.' So we put up the new sign bearing your name. It's been hanging there ever since."

"I don't understand. Why didn't he want to tell me?" Lauren looked around the unit. Everything in it was state of the art. Millions of dollars must have been invested into this asthma center.

Doug shrugged. "You know better than anyone how private Joe can be, especially when he feels strongly about something. But I also suspect that he wanted to leave a legacy of something positive, something that would continue to help others long after he was gone." He smiled. "I don't think he fully understood just how big an impact this center would have. Not only are we a referral center for patients from a much wider radius, we've also attracted some terrific young doctors. You know what a problem it can be to get good physicians to move to a small town. But apparently the word is getting out that this is a great place to live, quiet, within easy reach of big cities but still holding on to its small-town charm. We've even got some new startup businesses moving here."

"I had no idea," Lauren said. *So, the old town's got life in it after all.*

"And the most exciting news is, due to the success and reach of the center, the hospital is expanding. We'll be breaking ground on a stand-alone short-stay surgery unit next year. The five-year plan also includes a birthing center."

"That's fantastic," Lauren said.

"I'll tell you, it's a great thing to see this old hospital catching up with the times. And in no small way, it all started with your father. His faith in this place. In this town. And the kindness of its people." He patted her shoulder. "Well, I have to keep on with my rounds. You probably want to get back to your dad?"

Tears rose in her eyes and choked her throat as she realized the simple truth it seemed everyone else around her had always known: Joseph Keller was a truly special man.

"Just amazing," she said aloud, for the first time knowing the truth about her father. For the first time, *knowing* her father. What a legacy he would leave his town, his family . . . and his daughter.

Lauren walked slowly back down the stairs, heading back to the ICU.

***

Later that afternoon, Lauren sat with her mother in the hospital café. "I'm feeling so guilty now, Mom," Lauren said. "I wish I had found all this out about Dad years ago. I still don't understand why he wouldn't let you tell me why we moved to Hope."

Audrey nodded. "We discussed it quite a bit, but as usual I gave in to him. Maybe I did that too much," she said reflectively. "I'm old fashioned, Lauren, you know that. I still believe the man should be the head of the household. Over the years, I've certainly become more assertive, of course. And my counseling work has taught me that a good marriage *has* to involve give-and-take. Even if one person is naturally a take-charge personality, that doesn't mean they are always right. Sometimes they need to give way, for the good of both people and the relationship."

That's aimed at me, Lauren thought. But for now, her marriage wasn't what she wanted to talk about.

"I didn't understand. I thought he didn't care about me anymore, about my dreams, by dragging me away from my life in DC. But he did. And I thanked him by moving away. And pushing him away. I wish I could go back in time and—"

Audrey caught her hand and stopped her.

"Don't do that. Regrets are a waste of time. We make choices with the best available information at the time, based on the circumstances. And your father didn't mind. Truly he didn't."

"How could he not mind that I was so focused, even obsessed with my career and that you two hardly ever saw me?"

"Well, of course, he wanted to see you more often. We both did. But no, he didn't mind that you were so busy. He wanted you to follow your dreams. He loved you so much that your happiness and fulfillment were more important to him than his own. The question is, Lauren, *are* you happy and fulfilled?"

Chapter Twenty-Four

BEFORE LAUREN COULD ANSWER, her cellphone rang. Making an apologetic face at her mother, she answered it.

"Lauren," said Anna Novotny. "How are things?"

Lauren stood and moved away from her mother, not wanting Audrey to overhear as she quickly updated Anna on Joe's status.

"I'm sorry to hear that," Anna said, and she sounded sincere. "Is he stable, though?"

"For the moment."

"I hate to do this, but you told me you hoped to be back in Boston tomorrow. Is there any chance you can be here in time for a meeting with me at eight in the morning? We need to talk, and I'd rather do it face-to-face."

That doesn't sound good, Lauren thought, but she said only. "Yes, I guess I can fly back tonight."

"Good. Let's meet first thing tomorrow, then. My office?"

Lauren agreed, hoping her trepidation didn't reveal itself in her voice, and hung up. Turning back to her mother, she explained that she had been called back to Mass General and that she had to leave right away.

"But it's good. I can meet with the specialist there and find out if there's anything else we can do for Dad. I'll be back as soon as I can.

By tomorrow evening, probably," she promised. She gave her mother a strong hug. "Explain to Chris and Joey that I'm doing this for Dad, okay?" She pulled up an app on her phone and made a reservation on the evening puddle-jumper to Philadelphia and for a connecting flight to Boston.

**

As she drove through the town streets, it seemed to her that the town looked different. She felt like she was seeing Hope for the first time. The little downtown area had more boutique-type shops and restaurants than she remembered, and people were queuing outside the old local playhouse, whose Art Deco facade had been spruced up. Many others seemed to be just enjoying a stroll along the sidewalks in the pleasant June evening. *It really is a pretty town.*

As she drove away from the downtown area, she admired the well-kept rowhouses that lined the pleasant boulevards. Many had tidy gardens. Suddenly she remembered her father telling her, "Every garden is unique. A yard reflects the personality of the owner. My best work are the gardens I put in for people that I know. I try to use plants and flowers that personify the owner. I want them to be able to see themselves in their garden and also have a sanctuary in which they can find refuge. That's my goal, Rennie, to bring solace to people."

Such a goal had seemed trivial to her back then. But now, she knew what he meant.

It seemed to her that she could guess which yards her father worked on. They were the ones carefully landscaped with a variety of plants of many sizes, shapes, and colors, as opposed to the ones with a thin strip of standard annual flowers along the walkway.

Joe would make monthly trips to different states and bring back unique plants to store in his small greenhouse in the backyard. Sometimes, he would make it into a family outing, a weekend away, but the older Lauren got, the less willing she was to go. She had other things to do. She was too busy memorizing chemical compounds and working out physics problems to be wasting time digging holes. When she wasn't studying, she was working at the library, trying to make enough money for college. But Joe never stopped asking.

When she got to Mrs. Boudreaux's house, she stopped the car. She wanted to see the place where her father had last been awake. As she stared around the yard, she noticed a white azalea bush lying on its side, partly hidden from the street by a droopy Japanese maple. On impulse she got out of her car and walked into the yard. There was a hole already dug for the plant. *Is this the bush Dad was planting when he had his stroke?* She knelt, picked up the bush, and placed it gently into the hole. Reverently, she pushed the loose dirt in around the plant, tamping it down firmly. Standing up and brushing her hands off, she took a few steps back and regarded her work.

"It is a pretty bush," she said aloud.

"Yes, it is," a voice said from the porch.

Lauren turned around. "Oh, Mrs. Boudreaux. It's me, Lauren Keller. I'm sorry. I didn't mean to trespass. I just wanted to finish my father's work."

"My word, look at you, Lauren," said the old lady, smiling at her. Her corona of fluffy white hair resembled the azalea flowers Joe had picked out for her. "I remember you when you were in pigtails. You have grown into quite a lovely woman. I'm so sorry about your father. I feel just awful about it," she said in a shaking voice. "I found him, you see, but they tell me he was here for hours. I just can't forgive myself for not finding him earlier."

"Please don't say that, Mrs. Boudreaux. Dad was doing what he loved. If it wasn't here, it would have been somewhere else," Lauren told her. "Finding him earlier probably wouldn't have made much difference to his condition," she admitted to herself as much as to the older woman. "It isn't your fault. You know Dad would hate to think of you feeling bad."

Mrs. Boudreaux nodded slowly. "Thank you for saying that." She looked at the bush. "I'd better water that. I can do that much. Ever since Freddy passed away three years ago, I just couldn't manage the yard by myself anymore. And your father does such wonderful work," she said with a smile. "Now my yard reminds me of my childhood growing up outside of Atlanta. Such happy times. I come out here every day and sit in my garden to listen to the birds. It has brought me so much peace," she continued. "Until now. I'll never be able to look at that bush without thinking about your father."

"But that's how it should be," Lauren said. "Think of him. Know that he put his heart and soul into your garden and every other one he created. In many ways, Mrs. Boudreaux, you have more of him than I do," she said sadly.

"Oh now, I doubt that very much, dear. But I did so enjoy talking with him. I would bring him iced tea, and he would tell me about all of you. About your little boy, Joey. My, how your daddy loved that child. He said you'd married a good man who was like the son he never had. And, of course, he told me about you. How hard you work in Boston. About all the wonderful things you do for your patients and all the suffering you relieve. He was so very proud of you, Lauren."

"Well, thank you," Lauren said. *I know. I now know he was proud of me.* "I'm so sorry, but I have a plane to catch."

"Oh, yes. But before you go," Mrs. Boudreaux said, pulling her wallet out of her purse, "please take this. It's what I owe him, even if that stubborn man said he got more in cookies and iced tea than his work was worth."

Lauren let out a chuckle. "No, ma'am," she answered, raising her hands in protest. "If my father didn't take your money, I'm certainly not going to. I'm sure your cookies were more than enough."

Mrs. Boudreaux insisted, but Lauren stood firm. "I see you are just like him," the old lady said with a wink, putting the money back.

If only that were true, Lauren thought. She waved goodbye, got back in her car, and headed for the airport. A wave of sadness overcame her as she drove past the sign on the edge of town. It was the first time she really noticed the old placard, and she wondered how long it had been there. She could barely read the faded writing that beckoned to her like a beacon on a stormy night: *Thank you for visiting Hope. Please come again!*

"I will," Lauren said out loud. "I will."

CHAPTER TWENTY-FIVE

AS LAUREN WAITED TO change planes in Philadelphia, it occurred to her that it would be nice to bring Joey for a visit to the historic city, even just for the day to see Independence Hall and the Liberty Bell. Maybe Chris would come. A weekend would be even better. They could take their time driving back up to Boston. Make a little vacation out of it.

The commuter flight from Philly to Boston was packed; Lauren had only been able to get a middle seat. But the flight was short, and her thoughts kept her occupied. The flight landed at Logan Airport a little after 9:30, and Lauren was wide awake. She pulled her car out of the long-term parking and drove to Massachusetts General instead of going home.

It was raining hard in Boston, and Tobin Bridge was backed up with bumper-to-bumper traffic, so it was past ten before she actually reached her office. The custodial staff were hard at work in the hallways, which were otherwise quiet. She let out a sigh when she saw the large stack of files that were placed in the middle of her desk. Chartwork. It always seemed to pile up, even after being away for just two days.

Then she noticed, strategically placed on the top of the stack on her desk, a memo from the hospital attorneys asking her to write a rebuttal letter for the complaints lodged by Dr. Sutton. "Tomorrow," she said aloud in defiance to the empty room as she put the memo aside and picked up the first chart.

She had barely made a dent in the stack when she heard, "Why, Lauren," from the doorway. "I didn't expect you to get here tonight."

She turned to see Anna Novotny staring at her. The new DCS was dressed in a raincoat and carried an umbrella and briefcase, clearly on her way out.

"Yeah, well, I got into Logan early, and, well—" she trailed off.

"Well," Anna echoed. "We could have our meeting now, if you like? It won't take long."

Lauren nodded. *Might as well get it over with.*

Anna sat. "I wanted to give you give you the news, first. Lauren, I'm giving the Internal Medicine chair position to Dr. Hernandez." She eyed Lauren for her reaction. When Lauren said nothing, Anna went on. "I owe it to you to explain my choice. Lauren, you're one of the best diagnosticians I know. And you're organized and clear-thinking."

But, Lauren thought, waiting for it.

"But this position requires a person who is good at managing different personalities. And I'm afraid that's not you," Anna said quietly. "Quite frankly, you've ticked off a lot of the staff here over the past several years. It's not that you're were always necessarily wrong. On the contrary, you were usually right. But it's *how* you tell them that you're right that causes the friction. This complaint from Dr. Sutton only confirms a lot of people's opinions that you shouldn't be put in charge of the staff. I'm your friend, but I have to make the right decision for the hospital as a whole." Again, she peered closely at Lauren to see how she was taking the news.

Lauren sat, wondering at her own reactions. Part of her was upset and hurt. But her strongest reaction—relief. A little voice said, *This could be the best thing for me and my family.*

"I understand," she said. "I think you've made the right decision, Anna."

"You're not upset?" Anna asked.

"Oddly, I'm not. Truly." Lauren gave Anna a rueful grin. "It's been an interesting couple of days," she told her boss. "All of a sudden I'm questioning all my priorities."

Anna sighed with relief. "Well, that makes things easier for me. To be honest, I think you're better off staying out of administration. I thought it was hard enough juggling all those egos in the Internal Medicine department. It's ten times worse now at the directorate level. Most of my workday has nothing to do with practicing medicine."

"That would drive me crazy," Lauren agreed.

Anna smiled and stood. "I'm glad you recognize that. Your skills are needed on the wards, not in meeting rooms." She sighed, looking at her watch. "I've not been home before ten this entire week. Will you be here for the staff meeting at nine? I'm making the announcement then."

"Sure, I'll be there," Lauren answered.

"Get some sleep."

As Anna nodded and walked away, Lauren was surprised by her own thoughts. *Is that how it would have been if I got the promotion? More and more nights working late with nothing to show for it? Powerful, but alone and bitter, always having to deal with egos and competition between people willing to sacrifice whatever it takes to get ahead? People like me?*

Suddenly disinclined to work, Lauren turned off the lamp on her desk. Following another impulse—*I seem to be acting from impulse most of the time lately*—she left the hospital and drove not to the apartment she'd been staying in, but to the home she and Chris had bought. As Lauren got out of the car, she marveled at the noise of the traffic along what most Bostonians would consider a quiet side street. She thought about waking up in Hope, everything quiet and still except for the soft chirping of the birds in the maple tree her father had planted outside her bedroom window many years ago. *Did he do it on purpose? Did he want me to wake up to the soothing sounds of nature every morning?*

Yes, she was certain Joe Keller knew exactly what he was doing.

***

Lauren threw her keys on the small table beside the front door and walked into the dark living room, where she sagged onto the stylish couch she had purchased when they first moved in. Chris had wanted a cozier living room where the family could sit together, relax and enjoy family time. But Lauren argued that the living room should be elegant, a place she could entertain colleagues.

She shifted, trying to get more comfortable. She hadn't noticed previously how hard and cold the designer couch was. It was elegant, indeed, but not the most comfortable piece of furniture they owned. A noise startled Lauren, the sound of ice falling from the automatic ice maker over the hum of the refrigerator. Another sound, this time from the heating unit as it kicked in, forcing warm air through the vents. The rain must have caused the temperature to drop enough to trigger the thermostat.

Annoyed and unable to concentrate, Lauren stood and turned on the lights, looking at her so-called living room. *It's so sterile,* she thought. It was almost as if no one lived there. There was very little personality in the room at all. *Is that a reflection on me?*

Things were different in the kitchen, where she knew Chris and Joey spent most of their time. Even though it was as modern as the living room, the men in her family left their distinct imprints on the room—drawings on the refrigerator, books and a half-finished board game on the small wooden table in the dining nook, a vase of sweet pea flowers from the garden on the counter. Every time they visited Hope, Joey's grandfather gave them a plant for their own garden, and Chris dutifully took Joey out back to plant it when they returned to Boston. *But maybe it wasn't duty*, Lauren thought. *Maybe Chris likes gardening. My son too.* She recalled Joey's excitement when he'd brought in the first tomatoes from the garden last summer.

Lauren sat at the dining nook table and stared monotonously at the game board. Her drive to succeed had been inherited from her father. But he changed. He got his priorities straight. Ever since then he had been trying to show her a better way. He hadn't articulated it, but her father was not the kind of man who said things in words.

"He said it with flowers," she mouthed to the empty house. "And I couldn't hear the message. Until now."

Was it too late? She knew she was close to losing her husband and son. She wouldn't let that happen. *I'm Joe Keller's daughter*, she thought, straightening up. *Like him, I will do the right thing for my family.*

Chapter Twenty-Six

LAUREN AWOKE. SHE'D FALLEN asleep on the couch, uncomfortable as it was, and managed to sleep fitfully until six. Her lids were heavy and her eyes ached. *Not enough REM sleep*, she self-diagnosed. Lack of enough time in the deepest state of sleep, the dream state, meant she was not restored.

Slowly she rose from the couch and made her way methodically to the bathroom. A shower helped clear her head a bit, as did the half pot of coffee she drank after she got dressed. Although most of her things were in the apartment, she kept some items here for when she came to spend time with Chris and Joey on the weekends. She found a pair of black slacks in the bureau, but the only top she found to wear was a sleeveless sea-green, V-necked blouse her mother had sent her. She'd never cared for it; it looked more like vacation wear than something a professional woman wore to the office. But looking in the mirror, she had to admit that the color was flattering.

She rarely spent much time staring in the mirror. She'd never thought much of her looks. Her mother was the family beauty, while Lauren took after her father, with strong features. But as she examined her reflection, she saw a striking woman, a woman in the prime of life whose defined cheekbones and chin promised she would remain attractive even in old age.

The short, efficient haircut she'd worn for years wasn't doing her any favors, though. *Maybe I'll grow my hair longer,* she thought. *That would make Chris happy.*

***

Back at the hospital, the stack of folders was still waiting. As she worked through the charts, she thought about how her life could so easily be this and nothing more. Waking up in an empty apartment, separated from her family, working from dawn to dusk for people that didn't care about her, only what she could do for them.

The chart work done, she picked up the legal memo and read the complaint. She had to admit it did give a relatively accurate description of her conduct. Although Dr. Sutton was specifically referring to the encounter on the wards several days ago, it could have been any day in Lauren's professional life. *Disregard for other people's feelings; humiliating physicians in front of staff and patients; threatening; bitter; harsh; uncaring; cold and callous; vindictive.*

That was Lauren Keller as many saw her. But that wasn't who she wanted to be. It wasn't who she was deep down inside. Was it? She doubted that Doug Spiva ever had anything so horrible written about him. In fact, she doubted that Dr. Spiva had ever had a legal case brought against him. Patients who respected and liked their physicians rarely sued.

Lauren closed the folder. She took a deep breath and stood up, reaching over her desk to pick up the picture of herself, Chris, and Joey taken at Christmas. She stared at it for a long time.

Her phone rang. "Dr. Keller," she answered crisply, although she felt anything but sharp that morning.

"Lauren. I'm glad I caught you," said the deep, slightly accented voice of Dr. Hans Jurgesson. "I was hoping you were back."

"Hans, good to hear from you."

"Do you have time to join me in about fifteen minutes?"

"Of course, I'll be right there."

The hospital was bustling at seven thirty in the morning. Residents scurried though the halls gathering every bit of information on their patients to present to their attending within the hour. Nurses took vitals and attended to patients.

The Department of Radiology's main reading room was enormous, with dozens of workstations set up in small cubicles in the center of the large, dimly lit room. Here, radiologists read hundreds of X-rays, MRIs, CTs, ultrasounds and other electronic and magnetic investigations into the human body every day.

In a corner, surrounded by team of young physicians, Dr. Hans Jurgesson was walking a group of medical students through the pathology of Alzheimer's disease.

"These indicators," he explained as he pointed to a positron emission tomography image, commonly called a PET scan, "show the progressive loss of brain function in Alzheimer's. The blue color reflects areas of reduced activity, signaling degenerative changes in the brain. These red images, however, highlight the neural structures are still intact and functioning. It's an incredibly powerful tool." Hans paused when he noticed Lauren standing patiently behind his students. "That can help us decide which treatment protocols to consider to slow the progression of this debilitating disease. Dr. Cho, would you please pull up the next set of films and lead the discussion?"

"Of course, Doctor," the senior radiology resident replied. Hans made his way around his students to meet Lauren.

"Hi, Lauren. Thank you for coming here." He lowered his voice. "I thought perhaps it would be helpful for you if we went over your father's case together, in detail. Just so you have no doubts or questions."

"Thank you," Lauren said. "I appreciate your time on this busy day."

They went into a private consultation room. Dr. Jurgesson methodically pulled up the scans sent by Nurse Maureen in the ICU back in Hope, taking time to quietly analyze each picture. He was exceedingly thorough. Even the pictures of parts of Joe's brain unaffected by the stroke were subject to intense scrutiny by Dr. Jurgesson. After every image had been thoroughly examined, he turned to face her.

"Well, Lauren. You already realize the severity of his stroke," he said softly as he took off his glasses. There was a deep sympathy in his eyes. "The damage to the tissue is extensive. Whatever we might try won't change that. Even if he lives, he won't get much function back. I'm sorry to be so brutally blunt, Lauren, but I'd want the same if it was my father."

"No, you're right. Tell me your honest opinion. Please. I need to hear it."

"Look at the damage," continued Hans, pointing to the darkened areas on the scans. "You know what this means. His neocortex is gone, Lauren. It's just his brainstem keeping him alive. I can't see him waking up from this."

Lauren stared at the images of her father's brain on the computer screen.

"I'm so sorry. Has he left directions?"

"He has a DNR, but nothing else is specified," Lauren answered, referring to the Do Not Resuscitate legal document. "My mother has his medical power of attorney and can make decisions for him."

"What would your father want?"

Lauren found her eyes filling with tears. "He wouldn't want to go on like this," she admitted. "Not just for himself. He wouldn't want my mother, or any of us, to have the burden of caring for him when there was no hope," she went on, knowing it was true. Joe Keller, who had shouldered so many burdens in his time—sometimes literally, carrying someone out of danger as he had done with Harry—would never want to be a burden to others.

But I would do it, she thought. *I would carry that burden. We all would: Mom, Harry, Mike, Doug. We owe him that.*

It was a conundrum doctors witnessed every day. Whose wishes took precedence, the patient's or the family's? Although the law was clear, the ethics sometimes weren't. Lauren now understood for the first time why family members sometimes found it so hard to comply with the wishes of their loved ones that nothing be done to prolong life. *But it is what he wants. And we owe him that, as well.*

Lauren pulled herself out of her reverie to thank Hans for taking so much time for her. He surprised her with a quick hug. "Again, I'm so sorry," he said.

She nodded her thanks, then strode down the hall with her usual purposeful step, heading for Anna Novotny's office. There was one thing left for Lauren to do. And one phone call to make.

CHAPTER TWENTY-SEVEN

LAUREN'S FLIGHT TOUCHED DOWN in Philadelphia at noon. By now, Anna Novotny would have announced that Dr. Luis Hernandez was the new chair of Internal Medicine, and that Dr. Lauren Keller had taken a leave of absence. Some of the staff would speculate about the connection between the two, especially since Lauren didn't stay for the meeting. But Lauren didn't care. She had more important matters on her mind.

Her ten-minute meeting with Anna before leaving Boston was brief and to the point. Lauren needed time and would not be returning to her position at Mass General anytime soon—if ever again. She had other priorities to focus on right now.

On the small commuter plane that hopped from Philadelphia to Hope, Lauren contemplated how she was going to make things work. It was going to be difficult, for sure. She had to find a way to convince both Chris and Joey to give her another chance. And there were other things she needed to set in motion.

When she passed the *Welcome to Hope* sign, she smiled. *Home, again.* She headed straight to the hospital.

Chris's pickup was in the hospital's small parking lot, as was her mother's car and Uncle Harry's Lexus. No doubt Mike Laurence's car—*Bet it's a 4x4 of some type*—was somewhere close by. Sure enough, there was a Chevy Tahoe with Virginia plates parked beyond the Lexus.

"Good. They're all here. That'll make it easier."

She parked and entered the hospital, making a beeline for the ICU. But when she walked into her father's room, she wasn't emotionally prepared for what she saw. Friends and family were packed into the small room or standing in the doorway. *Paying their respects to a great man.* No one noticed Lauren as she stood at the door because all eyes, moist with tears, were on the littlest person in the room.

"I wrote this poem for you, Poppy. I hope you like it," Joey said quietly. The people crammed into the space made no sound; the only noise came from the beeping of the cardiac monitor attached to Joe's chest, slowly rising and falling as the respirator kept him alive.

> *You took me to my first ball game, and we had a good time,*
> *Your team lost but mine won, and that was just fine.*
> *Baseball season's here again, and we need to go see,*
> *I'll even root for your team, just come back home to me.*
> *I miss working with you in your garden, we always have fun,*
> *Planting your flowers and bushes and playing in the sun.*
> *Get better, Poppy, I need you to come home,*
> *It's quiet in your house, I feel all alone.*
> *I'm taking care of your garden, I planted another seed,*
> *Just get well soon, I'll do whatever you need.*

After he finished reading the words written on the back of a paper napkin liberated from the hospital cafeteria, Joey took his Philadelphia Phillies cap off his head and placed it under his grandfather's still hand.

Some of the visitors walked out of the ICU, stifling sobs. Lauren made her way through the crowd, knelt down, and hugged her son tightly. Now, she knew for sure that she was making the right decision. It would be all right, no matter what happened today.

"Honey, that was so beautiful. I'm sure Poppy loved your poem," she told him, holding him close.

"Mommy, you came back! Do you think he heard it?"

"Yes, Joey. I do," she answered. "And yes, I came back. I'm not leaving you again."

Chris walked over and put a hand on her shoulder.

"Welcome back," he said to his wife.

Lauren took his hand and stood up. They exchanged a long look. At first, Chris looked curiously at his wife, then smiled tentatively. He sensed something was different.

"What did your doctor friend say about your father?" Audrey asked.

Lauren reached out and took her hand too. "I'm so sorry, Mom," was all she said.

Audrey swallowed. "I didn't really, but I—" She broke down. Harry and Joanna put their arms around her and held her as she wept.

Joey looked at his family. "What's wrong? Isn't Poppy going to get better?" he asked, his lower lip quivering.

Chris picked Joey up and held him. Lauren stroked the boy's hair.

"No, honey, he's not. He's too sick to get better. There's nothing anyone can do."

"I don't want him to die!" the boy protested. "I hate this place! I hate hospitals!"

Lauren put her arms around him and Chris, willing comfort to the child facing death for the first time in his life.

Dr. Spiva's voice came from behind her. "I think we need to let Joe's family have some time alone with him," he said to the crowd. One by one, the visitors filtered out, each touching Joe on the hand or bending down to whisper something to him as they left. Some left notes for him, others placed tokens of remembrance beside the bed. Mike patted Lauren on the shoulder as he passed by.

Brother, wife, daughter, grandson, sister-in-law, and son-in-law stood solemnly, looking at Joe. "He looks at peace," Audrey said quietly, wiping her eyes. "It's strange. I met your poppy in a hospital, did you know that?" she asked Joey.

"Was he sick?" the little boy asked, the tears still running down his cheeks.

"No, he was there to help people. So was I." She smiled sadly at Joey. "Yes, people do go to hospitals when they're sick. But most of the people in the hospital are there to help the sick people. Like your mommy does."

"I know," sniffled Joey. "But—"

"But it's hard when they can't," Lauren said softly. "It's the hardest thing ever, wanting to help and not being able to." She looked around at her family. "We're a family of helpers and healers. You too, Joey. Even right now, you're upset that you can't help Poppy. But you know what? I am so proud of you for wanting to. Your poppy is proud too," she added. "Always remember that."

**

Hours later, Lauren sat with Chris in the cafeteria. Joey, worn out with crying, was asleep in Lauren's lap. It would take him time to accept what was happening. But he had a loving family to help him through his sorrow. *He'll be fine*, Lauren thought, looking at him. *I'll make sure of it.*

"You know," she told Chris, "that I have spent my entire life living in books, pursuing every bit of knowledge I could find. While other kids played with dolls or at sports, I went to the library and read. I've learned something new this week, though, and it wasn't from any book. My father, who I thought didn't do much with his life, has been living such a full life while I only studied it from afar, afraid of living it like he did. For all this knowledge I supposedly gained, I've been pretty stupid."

Chris shook his head, smiled, but said nothing.

"Knowledge just doesn't come from books," she continued, looking down at her young son. "My father wasn't a book-smart man. He never went to college. But his wealth of experience meant more than all those facts I memorized out of the mounds of books I've pored through in my life." She sighed.

Chris stirred. "I wouldn't say that. You help so many people with your knowledge. Save lives. There are many types of wisdom, Lauren. Your father had a special kind, but so do you. Don't downplay your hard work and all who benefit from it."

Is this my husband talking? The man who wanted me to stop working so hard?

Lauren shrugged as she replied. "Maybe. But people remember Dad not only for what he did, but for who he was, the kind of person he was toward others. I'm finally getting this." She looked up at Chris, seeing the concern for her in his eyes, and smiled at him. "After all these years, I finally understand my father. And that means I understand myself. I'm not being hard on myself. I'm owning up to my mistakes so I can correct them before it's too late. I hope it's not too late for me and Joey. Or for me and you," she said.

"Where's all this coming from?" Chris asked.

"Over the past two days, I learned more about my father than I ever knew about him, my entire life. Everywhere I've gone in this town, people have told me stories of his compassion, generosity, selflessness, and love. He's such a good man. Always was. I was just too blind and self-absorbed to see it." She took a breath. "But I can learn from his example. We can be a family again, Chris. I think I know how to do that now. Through my actions and through my life. That's what my father was always trying to tell me. The kind of man my father was, that's the kind of person I'll strive to be. To walk in his footsteps."

Joey stirred in her arms. "Are you and Daddy going to stop fighting and be happy?" he asked.

Lauren dropped a kiss on top of his head. "Yes, I think we can. I hope we can." She looked back at her husband. "Chris, I love you. I appreciate everything you've ever done for me and Joey. I can't bear the thought of losing either of you. I'll never let work come between us again. I promise," she said, with all the sincerity she could muster.

"Wow, Lauren. It's been a long time since I've heard you say you appreciated me," Chris said softly.

"Well, you'll not only hear it from me, but also see it in my actions from now on," she said. "I'll not take my family for granted ever again. Nor will I let life pass us by. We'll enjoy it together." She met his eyes. "If you'll give me a second chance."

Chris got up, came around the table, and knelt by her, putting a hand on her knee. "Lauren, of course I want us to be a family again," he said. "But I have to ask. How will you do that and keep up all your obligations at Mass General, at Harvard? Have you thought about that?"

"Yes," Lauren replied. "I've thought quite hard about that. Right before I left Boston, I called Doug Spiva to ask a favor. Chris, there's a place for me at this hospital."

Chris's jaw dropped. "You would quit Mass General?" he asked.

"I'm on leave as of today. But it's up to you and Joey. If you want to move to Hope, then I'll make it final." She smiled at Chris. "You already work from home; you can keep doing that from Hope, if you want to. But Doug tells me there's a new startup company in town that's looking for someone with your skills,

and he would be happy to connect you. We could work out our schedules so that I can be home with Joey afternoons that you work. I'd actually like that."

Chris broke into a huge grin. "Lauren, I can hardly believe my ears. It sounds perfect."

"What do *you* think? Would you like to live here in Hope?" she said, looking down at Joey.

"Yes!" Joey yelled loudly, jumping up and dancing. "I love it here! Yay!" He saw the other people in the room looking at him and subsided. "Oops, sorry, I forgot to use my inside voice."

"It's okay, Joey," his father said. "I think we're all pretty excited." He stood and pulled Lauren to him for a kiss.

"Well, I'm feeling a bit left out. How about a hug, Joey?" said

Audrey from behind them.

Joey whirled around and quickly complied as his parents, still holding each other tightly, looked on. "We're moving here, Nana! I can see you all the time now!"

"That's wonderful!" Audrey replied. She looked at Lauren. "I'd love to hear all about this. But I came to tell you that Harry and Joanna just left and no one else is in the room with your father. Do you want to spend some alone time with him?"

"Yes, Mom, I do. We'll talk later," Lauren replied. She smiled at Chris and gave him a quick peck on the cheek before walking away.

As she went, she heard her mother ask, "Joey, have you had anything to eat yet?"

"Not yet, Nana. Can I have some pizza? And ice cream after?"

"Sure. My treat. What's being a grandmother good for if I can't spoil you?"

***

"Dad, it's Rennie," Lauren said, her voice cracking as she entered Joe's hospital room and knelt by his bed. "I'm back. Back to stay."

She gazed upon the man lying so quietly. Then she made a sign of the cross and prayed to God as she had not prayed in years. But it wasn't enough to confess her sins to God. In a low voice, still holding Joe's hand tightly, she said, "Dad, I'm so sorry. I've been such a fool. I made all these assumptions about you, not realizing that you spent your life trying to do the best for me and for Mom and for everyone around you. That you always put me first, even when I couldn't see it. That you always loved me, even when you couldn't be there, even when you couldn't tell me. I understand you now. I'm sorry it took me so long. I'm sorry I didn't get the chance to tell you until now, when it's too late. That I love you."

She put her head on her father's chest and cried. She cried long and hard, allowing all of the emotions she had repressed her entire life to pour out freely.

Then she felt it. Did her father's finger twitch ever so briefly?

Had he heard her? Was he trying to communicate with her? If only he had heard her, if only he knew the tremendous impact he had on her life. That she loved him. She knew it wasn't possible. The damage was too extensive. It was her imagination.

She raised her head and stared at him. Around the medical tape and intubation tube, she thought, only for a second, that she saw his lips curved ever so slightly into a tiny smile. Then his face relaxed back into stillness. Had he heard her? Although all the science she had memorized over the decades told her it couldn't be true, her heart hoped that somewhere deep inside, her father was still there and had heard her confession. And now, he was at peace.

***

At exactly 3:37, Joe Keller died. The sky was clear. Its deep, rich blue arched over Hope as the sun warmed the grounds outside the hospital. No matter what was happening in ICU bed number three, it was a beautiful day, the kind of day Joe Keller loved.

Although Joe's vital signs were monitored closely by nurses at their station, all they could do was watch as his heart slowed down. With permission from the family, Dr. Spiva had turned off the respirator. Slowly, Joe's natural breaths became shallow and then stopped. On one side of his bed sat the love of his life, his soulmate, who, for the last time, had seen her husband through another difficult time. The other important woman in Joe's life stood on the other side of the bed.

"He's gone," Lauren said softly. Chris, standing next to her, held Joey close. Mike Laurence put a strong arm around his best friend's widow. Harry and Joanna stood at the foot of the bed, arms around each other.

With trembling hands, Lauren removed the intubation tube. She brushed her father's hair and kissed his forehead.

"I'll miss you, Dad. Thanks for always being there for me, even when I didn't know it. I love you so much," she whispered into his ear as she hugged him for the last time.

Chapter Twenty-Eight

THE BELLS OF SAINT Mary's Catholic Church rang out for all to hear. It seemed to Lauren that the entire population of Hope was packed into the church, leaving only standing room for the unlucky few who arrived late to the funeral.

The priest stood by the altar, facing his flock. It was difficult to see Father O'Malley through the many floral arrangements that adorned the altar and front of the church, donated by dozens of people. Some were from florists, but many were obviously from home gardens, simple arrangements of love.

Audrey sat on the right side of the nave in the first pew, dressed in black but with a bright corsage of flowers. The tissues in her hand were already moist with tears. Lauren sat upright beside her mother, her arm around Audrey's shoulders for support. Chris and Joey sat next to Lauren. Harry and Joanna and their two sons, who had flown in from out-of-state to pay their final respects to their beloved uncle, filled out the pew. Dr. Doug Spiva and his family were in the next row. Behind them, Mike Laurence sat erect in full military uniform next to his wife, Becky.

Father O'Malley began the service, anointing the flag-draped casket with incense and oil after blessing all present. The service was a long one, but no one seemed to mind. All listened somberly as the elderly priest spoke about Joe, nodding as he praised the man he called his friend. When he finished, Father O'Malley nodded to Lauren.

She kissed her mother on the cheek and stood up, walking to the front of the church. As she looked out at the packed church, she saw many faces she'd come to know: old Mrs. Boudreaux, weeping openly; Beth sitting next to a young man who resembled her and must have been Pete, the brother Joe had helped; the waitress from the café; Maureen and the other staff from the hospital who had taken such good care of Joe in his last days. As her eyes traveled across the crowd, she saw a dozen or so men in uniform standing at the back. The Army was there to honor one of their own.

Lauren took a breath and began speaking to the crowd. "I am a woman who has achieved many things. My research has been published in top medical journals. I've contributed to medical textbooks. I worked for years at the most hallowed grounds of medicine, Massachusetts General Hospital in Boston. But I cannot hold a candle to the person my father was, to what he accomplished in his full, rich life.

"Although he never went to college and had little money, he was the wealthiest man I've ever known. For a man's worth is not a reflection of his treasures, his power or glory. Rather, it is the measure of his deeds, as well as the breadth and depth of his friendships.

"He was a true hero, in every sense of the word. Most of what he did in the service of his country cannot be told. But in truth, Dad wouldn't want us to remember him for that, anyway. He never wore the many medals he earned or even talked about his days as a soldier. Not that he wasn't proud of his military service. He had a deep love of his country and comrades-in-arms. But what he would want us to remember him for, I am sure, is the legacy he left behind here in Hope. He touched so very many people in his life. The large crowd here is a testament to my father's generous and caring nature, which we experienced through his gardens, his smile, his warmth, and most of all, his love. He *loved* every day of his life.

"Now the angels have carried him to heaven. While our lives may seem darker without him," she went on, smiling down at her family, "it is not an exaggeration to say the world is truly a brighter place because of Joseph Keller, on so many levels. Whether he gave us a new garden, a kind word, a warm hug, a helping hand, or a compassionate, understanding smile, he made our lives better as a result.

"During the past few weeks, with the help of many of you, I finally got to know my father for the man he truly was. History will not record Joseph Keller as a Nobel Prize winner, a world leader, or a man of material wealth or power. He was so much more than all of those things. He never compromised his values and was steadfast in his beliefs. While he didn't seek out trouble, he stood strong for what he believed in and never backed away from evil. He was a compassionate man you could trust and count on. He was always there when needed, fought for what he thought was right, and protected what he loved. He defended his men while in the military and did all he could to make this town a better place after he retired. Most of all, he loved his family and took care of us. At all costs.

"Learning about my father made me realize what it really takes to be a loving daughter, a loving parent, a loving spouse . . . a good person. I only wish I can achieve a fraction of the success he had in his life. With him watching over me and guiding me, I'll do my best to live up to his legacy. Dad, I love you and will miss you always."

The vaulted nave of the cathedral echoed back sounds of hushed weeping evoked by Lauren's heartfelt words. Lauren returned to her seat and sat quietly reflecting as Doug, Chris, Mike, and Harry stood up to join Hope's mayor and the chief of police, carrying Joe's flag-draped coffin down the aisle to the waiting hearse.

Mike had offered to make the arrangements for Joe to be buried in a military cemetery or even Arlington, but Joe's will was specific. Years ago, he had purchased the two plots next to his mother's grave in Hope. Joe was to be laid to rest in one, while the other lay waiting for his wife to join him.

Six police cars escorted the funeral procession to the small cemetery outside of town. The mayor himself drove Audrey, Lauren, Chris, and Joey in his town car behind the hearse, at the head of a long line of cars flowing through and shutting down the still streets of Joe's hometown. As the procession rolled to a stop at the covered gravesite, a military escort marched smartly up to the rear of the hearse and reverently removed the casket of their fallen comrade from the vehicle, carrying it to Joe's final resting place.

After a few more words and a thoughtful prayer from Father O'Malley, another team of soldiers stood at the ready with their M-16 rifles. The twenty-one-gun salute startled most of the mourners, but little Joey's eyes shone and he whispered, "Cool!" under his breath. The flag was removed from the top of the casket and folded with precision. Colonel Michael Laurence, United States Army, with rows of medals glinting in the bright sunlight, carried the flag to Audrey.

"From a grateful nation," he said to her. She took the flag, then hugged Mike. Lauren saw a tear flow down Mike's cheek as he stepped back and saluted Audrey and the flag.

The oak casket, shining in the sunlight, was lowered into the ground. One by one, the long procession filed by, each dropping a flower on top of the casket.

Then it was over. Lauren looked at her mother. For the first time, Audrey looked frail to her. *Don't worry, Dad. We'll watch over her*, she promised her father's spirit as Chris and Joey helped Audrey to the car, leaving Lauren alone with her father one last time. "From your little butterfly, Rennie. I've come home, Dad," she said softly, tossing a single white azalea onto the casket. Mrs. Boudreaux had cut the flower that morning from the bush Lauren finished planting for her father.

Audrey was waiting for her at the car.

"I want you to have this," she said to her daughter. "It's your father's wallet. He always carried a picture of you in it."

"My graduation picture," Lauren confirmed, pulling out the worn photo and looking at it. "I thought I knew so much when this was taken. I had no idea how much more I still had to learn." As she went to replace the photo, something fell out with a *clunk* as it hit the pavement. Audrey bent down to pick it up.

"What is it?" Lauren asked her mother.

"It's your father's St. Jude medal. Your grandmother gave it to him when he went to Vietnam. He believed it helped him get through his most difficult times. He wore it every day he was in the military," Audrey told her daughter. "Except once, towards the end of his career. He gave it to you when you were in the hospital in Baltimore."

"I remember," she said sadly, clutching the medal tightly. She'd kept it, but after they moved to Hope, she had stuffed it in a drawer and left it after she moved out years later, forgotten with other items she wished to leave behind. Obviously, her father had found it. *I'm sorry, Dad. Now I will value it as I should have before*, she thought.

"What is it?" asked Joey, jumping up and trying to see. Lauren handed the medal to Joey. "It's a St. Jude medal. It was Poppy's. It kept him safe when he was a soldier." She glanced at her mother, then said to her son, "Would you like to have it?"

"Cool!" exclaimed Joey. "I mean, yes, thank you. If I wear this, will Poppy watch over me?"

"Always," Lauren promised.

The house was packed with well-wishers. Food brought by friends and acquaintances weighed down every table and counter and filled the refrigerator. Before going in, Audrey and Lauren sat quietly for a minute on a rocking chair on the porch of the family home, looking out over the most beautiful garden in the town, a gift to a wife from a loving husband.

Lauren took out her father's wallet and opened it. Behind Lauren's medical school graduation picture, there was another picture, a photo of Joe cradling Lauren as a baby. The photo was old and had many creases. How many times had Joe taken the picture out to look at it in some foreign land or show it to a friend or a stranger? Lauren imagined her father looking at the picture as he drove away from the burning wreck of a plane and a helicopter in Iran, in the dangerous streets of Beirut, and in the intensive care unit at Johns Hopkins as he watched over his only child.

Carefully, Lauren put the picture of her as a baby in her father's arms into her own small wallet and put it back into her purse. She would buy a new wallet, she thought, as she went with her mother into her father's house. One with plenty of room for pictures of her family.